The Little Vampire on the Farm

Tony thought a week's holiday on a farm would be dreadfully boring – so he persuaded his friend Rudolph the Little Vampire to go too. Rudolph knows nothing about the country, so Tony has to look after him, especially when Dr Rummage, a local vampire hunter, turns up!

With his parents encouraging him to take unnaturally healthy exercise on the one hand, and Rudolph's misadventures causing endless problems on the other, Tony certainly doesn't have the peaceful and relaxed break his parents were so keen on.

Angela Sommer-Bodenburg is the author of three other popular books about the Little Vampire: *The Little Vampire*, *The Little Vampire Moves In*, and *The Little Vampire Takes a Trip*.

The Little Vampire

ON THE FARM

ANGELA SOMMER-BODENBURG

Translated by Sarah Gibson

Illustrated by Amelia Glienke

Hippo Books
Scholastic Publications Ltd.
London

Scholastic Publications Ltd.,
10 Earlham Street, London WC2H 9LN, UK.

Scholastic Inc.,
730 Broadway, New York, NY 10003, USA

Scholastic Tab Publications Ltd.,
123 Newkirk Road, Richmond Hill,
Ontario L4C 3G5, Canada

Ashton Scholastic Pty. Ltd.,
PO Box 579, Gosford, New South Wales, Australia

Ashton Scholastic Ltd.,
165 Marua Road, Panmure, Auckland 6, New Zealand

First published in West Germany by
Rowohlt Taschenbuch Verlag, 1983

First published in the UK by Andersen Press, 1985

Published in paperback by Scholastic Publications Ltd., 1986

This translation copyright © Andersen Press Limited, 1985
Original title Der kleine Vampir auf dem Bauernhof

ISBN 0 590 70443 5
All rights reserved

Made and printed by Cox and Wyman Ltd.,
Reading, Berks

Phototypeset in Palatino by AKM Associates (UK) Ltd,
Ajmal House, Hayes Road, Southall, London

This book is for Burghardt Bodenburg, who is heartily annoyed because Boris has overtaken him in the race to grow vampire teeth – and for Katja, who still has no gaps in her baby teeth.

Angela Sommer-Bodenburg

Contents

1

Country Air

'Isn't it pretty here!' exclaimed Tony's mother, putting her case down on the dusty ground right next to a dried-up cowpat, as Tony noticed with glee.

'Very pretty,' he growled, looking sullenly over towards the farmhouse. To think he was going to have to stay here for a whole week with his parents, who had picked out this stupid farm by themselves!

A holiday on the farm – how boring it sounded already! Of course they had not bothered to ask him whether he would like to spend a few days of his holiday among cows, pigs and poultry! He would be able to go for nice walks and ride the farm horses – and breathe in the fresh country air. Fresh country air – that was a laugh too!

'Anyway,' he said to his parents, 'you must be pretty disappointed about the fresh country air. It stinks round here!'

'It doesn't at all!' contradicted his mother. 'I think the air is wonderful. So invigorating! Quite different from the air back home in town. Don't you agree?' She turned to Tony's father.

'Yes, of course,' he replied.

'Even so, it stinks,' Tony persisted. 'The air may be healthy, but it stinks.'

His mother threw him a scornful look. 'I

didn't know you had such a sensitive nose. When I think of your friend, that Rudolph Sackville-Bagg . . . .'

'What about him?'

'Don't you remember how smelly his cloak was?'

Tony had to grin. 'That cloak was a hundred years old though,' he said proudly. 'Perhaps even older.' Teasingly he added, 'It's always like that with vampires.'

He knew quite well that his parents did not believe in vampires. Everything he told them about his friend, the Little Vampire, they took to be pure invention. That was why the least risky thing was to tell his parents the truth about anything to do with the Little Vampire, for then they were least likely to believe him. And it was the same this time.

'I know, I know, vampires,' said his mother irritably. 'Thank God we're in the country now. At last we'll have some peace from your endless vampires – vampires on the telly, vampires in the cinema, and in all your horrible books.'

'Oh?' Tony bit his lip. If only they knew that the Little Vampire had been staying on this very farm since the previous night . . . .

'I'll take the luggage over,' he said cheerfully. He picked up a suitcase and two bags, and carried them to the door of the farmhouse.

'Now why's he so enthusiastic all of a sudden?' he heard his father say.

'It's only because of his vampires,' came his mother's reply. 'He can't bear anyone else to say what they think of them.'

2

2

Rustic Decorations

Tony had a good opinion of vampires. At any rate, of Rudolph Sackville-Bagg and his little sister Anna, who lived with their vampire family in the Sackville-Bagg vault. But did vampires really live? wondered Tony. All day long they slept like corpses in their coffins. It was only when the sun went down that they woke up and left their coffins under cover of darkness to go off hunting – hunting for human blood!

Tony shuddered. Even here, in the little guest room, it made him feel funny to think of the vampires' favourite food – and of the Little Vampire's bloodthirsty relations: Frederick the Frightful, Thelma the Thirsty, Sabina the Sinister – and Aunt Dorothy, the worst of them all!

At that moment, there was a knock on his door. Tony gave a startled jump. 'Y-yes?' he said hesitantly. The door opened and his father came in.

'Oh, it's you,' said Tony, relieved. For a moment, he had really thought a vampire might be standing outside his door, even though that could not be possible, for it was only shortly after 11 o'clock in the morning.

'Mrs Herring wants to show us the farm,' announced Tony's father.

'I've still got to unpack.'

'Do you like your room?' asked Dad, looking round. Without waiting for Tony's reply, he declared, 'It's quite delightful!'

'Suppose so,' said Tony. The cupboard, with its handpainted rustic decorations, the old-fashioned bed and the flowery curtains at the window were not exactly to his taste!

'Did you know that Mrs Herring had done all the painting herself?'

'Hmmm,' said Tony indifferently.

'If only I'd had all this at your age! A holiday on a farm, and even a room of my own! Do you know where I used to go for my holidays?'

'No-o.'

'To Gravel Water, just near where we lived. We had to bicycle all the way there, and the only thing we got was tuppence for an ice cream.'

Tony groaned softly. When his dad started on with his old stories, it was best not to say anything, for that was the quickest way to make him shut up.

'There was no question of going right away. Nowadays, on the other hand, it has to be at least some kind of resort, preferably with a swimming pool and a disco.'

Exactly, agreed Tony to himself.

'But we can still have a simple holiday. Isn't that right, Tony?'

Tony muttered something unintelligible. Then he said, 'I like it here too.' He snapped the lid of his suitcase shut and put his satchel, in which he had hidden the Little Vampire's

4

second cloak under some school books, into
the cupboard.

'Now I'm ready.'

Tony the Sensitive

Mrs Herring was standing in the yard, chatting to Tony's mother. She was wearing riding boots and jodhpurs; she had short blond hair and, to Tony's mind, did not look at all like a farmer's wife.

'Are you happy with your room?' she asked.

Why did grown-ups always have to ask the same question!

Tony nodded. 'Yes.'

'In fact, it's Joanna's room,' she said, 'but when we have holiday guests, she sleeps with Jeremy in his room. It's not too girly for you?'

'Tony isn't sensitive about things like that,' declared Tony's mother. 'As a matter of fact, we have particularly tried to teach him respect for girls in the way we have brought him up.'

'I beg your pardon?' said Tony angrily. Why on earth should she want to know that? He was extremely sensitive about anything to do with girls!

'In any case, Jeremy and Joanna are staying with their grandparents this weekend,' explained Mrs Herring.

'What a pity!' declared Tony's father. 'Tony won't have anyone to play with.'

'I can take care of myself,' said Tony irritably. He could do quite well without Jeremy, who he knew only played with knights in armour. And Joanna wasn't his cup of tea, either – he had seen her briefly when he came to the farm with his parents the first time, to book the rooms.

'Are your children on holiday too?' asked Tony's mother.

'No, not till the week after next.'

Tony listened to this in surprise. Then at least he would have some peace during the early part of the day.

'So, now I'll show you all round the farm!' Mrs Herring opened a wooden door painted green. 'This leads to the cowsheds.'

Tony's parents followed her – as happy and excited as if they'd never seen a cow before! thought Tony scornfully. He trotted behind them more slowly. They would soon see that he was much too old for a holiday on a farm!

4

Cattle

Tony nearly burst out laughing inside the cowsheds: they stank so revoltingly of cow-dung, even though they were empty! There was only a grey cat, who sat on a wooden beam washing herself. Tony looked over at his parents with a certain mockery.

'Fantastic cows!'

'Did you think they'd spend the whole time in here?' asked Mrs Herring.

'Why not? They have to be milked after all.'

'Milked?' Mrs Herring began to laugh. 'We've only got bullocks. And they're out in the field at the moment.'

Tony realised he was going red. How was he supposed to have known that? And in any case, he was not the slightest bit interested in cattle.

'Haven't you got any other animals?' he blurted out.

'Of course we have.' Mrs Herring went over to a little wooden partition. 'Here's a wee lamb, that we're bringing up on a bottle. He's called Baldwin.'

Tony nearly exclaimed, 'How sweet!' but just managed to stop himself. It was only little kids who went all gooey over baby animals!

Tony's parents stroked the little lamb.

'Wouldn't you like to stroke him?' asked Mrs Herring.

'No,' he growled, and thrust his hands into his trouser pockets.

'Tony thinks he's too old for this kind of thing,' said his father.

'I do not!' retorted Tony. 'But it's the sort of thing only girls like.'

'I beg your pardon?' exclaimed his mother heatedly. 'You really have gone too far this time!'

Suddenly all the anger he felt about this holiday rose up in him.

'So what if it is a girly thing? Stroking animals, riding – girls think all that's fantastic. But I do not!'

He turned away quickly because he felt tears welling up in his eyes. He couldn't care less now if his parents were mad at him.

There was a painful silence. Then he heard his father ask: 'Perhaps there are some bats somewhere? Tony's crazy about bats and vampires, you know.'

'Bats? There are a couple over in the barn. Would you like to see them?'

'Oh no, I'd rather not!' exclaimed Tony's mother. 'I'd prefer, for once, to have nothing to do with vampires or bats for a whole week!'

Tony breathed a sigh of relief. He was pretty certain the vampire had hidden his coffin over in the barn.

'Jeremy is mad about knights in armour,' said Mrs Herring. 'Every child has a craze on something.'

'It's not the same thing at all!' exclaimed Tony – rather unwisely, as he realised at once.

9

Mrs Herring asked: 'Why isn't it the same thing?'

'Because –' Tony hesitated. He absolutely must not say the wrong thing.

'Tony believes in vampires,' his father said. 'He even has a friend whom he claims is a vampire.'

Mrs Herring laughed. 'Then I must be grateful that Jeremy only plays with toy models.'

Tony was seething furiously, but this time he kept control of himself. Let them laugh at him – it only meant they did not have the slightest idea!

5

The Hero of the Henrun

'It says in your brochure that you have pigs as well,' said Tony's mother. 'That's right, pigs for fattening,' confirmed Mrs Herring. 'But I'm afraid I can't show them to you just now. You will have to wait until my husband feeds them at six o'clock.'

Tony stood and yawned. Pigs – as if he were interested in them!

'But we could go and look at the hens,' said Mrs Herring. With a glance at Tony, she added: 'Perhaps you would like our peacock.'

'Perhaps,' said Tony in a bored voice.

But he was impressed in spite of himself when he saw the peacock lifting its tail-feathers to form a huge, magnificently coloured wheel. As it did so, it gave a cry which sent shudders right through Tony. Luckily, the henrun was surrounded by a high wire fence.

'It's an uncanny sound, don't you think?' remarked Mrs Herring. 'Sometimes it even wakes us up.'

'Does it call at night as well?' Tony could not help thinking of the Little Vampire, who only knew about life in a town. How scared he would be if that terrifying cry rang out at night! The fright might even make him have a crash and break a leg! Whatever happened, he must warn him when they met up that evening.

Apart from the peacock, there were chickens – thirty or more of them. Mrs Herring threw them a handful of corn and they came rushing over, cackling. His parents smiled. Tony just twitched the corners of his mouth contemptuously. He did not find hens amusing!

'Don't you like chickens?' asked Mrs Herring.

'Yes, I do,' answered Tony, 'when they're in a soup!'

'Tony!' exclaimed his mother, but Mrs Herring only smiled. She pointed to a little hut in the middle of the henrun. 'If you're so keen on chickens, you ought to take a look at the laying hens. They sit on their eggs in that little hut and brood.'

With these words, she opened the gate of the henrun and pushed Tony inside. Suddenly he found himself surrounded by a flock of hens. He hopped from one foot to the other, in sheer terror that they might peck him in the leg. Mrs Herring laughed.

'They won't do anything to you!'

'You can never tell!' retorted Tony. He had once seen a film in which birds attacked human beings, and the picture of those hacking beaks was still very vivid in his memory.

'He's not afraid of vampires – but hens are a different matter!' mocked his father from the other side of the fence.

Tony threw him a furious look. 'I'm just being careful!'

Slowly he made his way back to the gate. As he did so, he never let the hens out of his sight, just to make sure they did not get worked up into a frenzy as they had in the film. But the birds just scratched about in the sand and pecked at the corn. Fortunately, he had just about reached the gate when the peacock gave a cry – so loud and so shrill that Tony went dead-white. Shaking, he shut the gate behind him.

'The Hero of the Henrun!' teased his father.

Tony's face darkened. With long strides, he stalked over to an upright bar which stood on a patch of grass near the henrun, pulled himself up and perched on the top.

'It's all right for you to laugh!' he called.

'You'll soon get used to it all,' Mrs Herring put in, 'even to hens! Come on, now I'll show you the horses,'

'Horses!' repeated Tony unenthusiastically.

'Blackie, the one we ride, and her foal, Tinka.'

Tony hesitated. But he did not want to admit that he was afraid of horses too. 'Okay then,' he said. 'But the horses are the last things I am going to look at.'

'It'll be lunch time by then anyhow,' replied Mrs Herring.

6

Ride a Cock Horse

Tony jumped down from the bar and followed Mrs Herring and his parents. They stopped in front of a low wooden fence.

'Blackie!' called Mrs Herring.

To Tony's surprise, a white horse came up to the fence, followed by a little brown foal. While Mrs Herring was talking to the horses, Tony stood by and thought how daft it was to talk to horses as if they were humans! After a while, Mrs Herring took an apple from her pocket and held it out to Tony.

'Here, you can give this to Blackie!'

'Me?'

'Yes, Then she'll get to know you and it will be easier when you come to ride her.'

'But I don't want to ride.'

'You don't want to ride?' Mrs Herring was astounded. 'But all our holiday guests want to ride. You like sport, don't you?'

'Ye-es,' he drawled.

'Well then. Now come along and give Blackie her apple. She's getting impatient.'

Cautiously, Tony stretched out his hand. The horse's huge head come nearer – its mouth opened, Tony saw two rows of enormous teeth . . . . He couldn't help it: his hand shook and the apple fell onto the grass.

Mrs Herring picked it up and gave it to Blackie. 'Blackie doesn't bite,' she said. 'Do you, Blackie?' she went on, turning to the horse. 'You're the most patient and best horse on the farm.'

'It's the first time Tony's ever been on a farm,' explained Tony's mother.

'And the last!' said Tony decisively.

'Tony, please!' exclaimed his mother. It was very clear how much she disapproved of the way Tony was behaving.

'The first day is always the most difficult.' Mrs Herring seemed unruffled. 'You're bound to like it better tomorrow, and you'll have got used to your new surroundings. So – now you can have a little go at riding.' She studied Tony's clothing and nodded approvingly. 'Jeans and wellington boots – that's just right for riding.'

Tony threw an imploring look at his mother. After all, he was wearing his new pair of jeans. But all she said was: 'Didn't you hear what Mrs Herring said?'

'Okay, okay.' In that case, it would be her fault if he fell off the horse and broke his neck! Resigned to his fate, he followed Mrs Herring into the paddock. She took hold of Blackie's halter and smiled encouragingly at Tony.

'Up you get!'

'Without a saddle?'

'Yes. That way you'll get a better feel of the horse.'

From close up, the horse looked even more enormous. 'How am I supposed to get on?'

'You hold onto the mane and swing yourself up.'

16

'Will the horse stand still for that long?'

'Of course. In any case, I've got hold of Blackie.'

'On your heads be it!' called Tony to his parents, then he took hold of the mane and swung himself up onto the horse's back. It wasn't half as difficult as he had imagined. Once he was sitting on top, he could not help giving a triumphant grin.

He pressed his legs tight to Blackie's flanks and sat up straight, just as he had seen it done in cowboy films. Mrs Herring watched him.

'Not bad for a beginner,' she said. 'If you put your mind to it, you'll be quite a good horseman one day.'

'Do you think so?' Tony was flattered.

'I do indeed.'

But all at once, Tony wasn't so sure she was right, because after an enthusiastic 'Gee up there, Blackie!' the horse started to move. Tony had trouble not to fall off.

A quarter of an hour later, when he had firm ground under his feet once more, he walked stiffly back to his parents.

'You did very well!' his father praised him.

'Really?'

Mrs Herring came up and said slyly, 'This afternoon it will be your turn to ride, anyway.'

'Me?' cried Dad.

'And your wife too!'

His parents' disconcerted faces made up for everything Tony had been through that morning.

17

'Of course!' he said. 'All holiday guests go riding. Or didn't you hear that?'

7
Jeremy and Joanna

After lunch, Tony went to his room. Ostensibly to read; in fact, he was worn out from riding and from carrying the coffin around the night before. He threw himself down on the bed and just managed to pull off his boots. Then he was asleep.

Shortly after four, his mother knocked on the door.

'Dad and I are going riding now.'

'Just coming,' murmured Tony sleepily. He heard her going back across the passage.

The next thing he heard was his father's voice. 'Hey, sleepyhead!'

'I'm . . . just coming.' Tony opened his eyes and saw his father standing by the bed.

'Do you know how late it is? Half past five!'

'As late as that?' queried Tony in disbelief. So he must have gone back to sleep again after his mother had knocked on the door. What rotten luck! he thought, because he had not been able to watch his parents riding. It must have been quite a laugh!

'Did you fall off?' he asked.

'No.'

'What about Mum?'

'She didn't either.'

'What a pity.'

His father just smiled. 'Jeremy and Joanna have just arrived.'

Tony groped for his boots with his feet and put them on. 'And they want to play with me?'

'Jeremy wants to show you the barn. He knows some fantastic places to hide, or so he tells me.'

That gave Tony a fright. It had never occurred to him that Jeremy and Joanna might discover the coffin while playing in the barn. He made his way down to the yard as quickly as possible.

At the front door, he nearly ran into Mr Herring.

'You wanted to see the pigs I believe?' said Mr Herring.

'The pigs? No, I . . . .' Tony stopped. The longer he stood here talking, the more likely it was they would discover the coffin, and he must prevent that at all costs!

'I'll take a look at the pigs tomorrow!' he called, and ran off before Mr Herring had a chance to reply.

The door of the barn was only pulled to. It squeaked as Tony opened it. Cautiously, he took a couple of steps forward and then stopped.

The two small dusty windows near the door let in only the dimmest of light. In the gloom, everything looked strange and unreal: the farm implements, the tractor by the wall and the old cart. A simple set of steps without a handrail led upwards. Full of foreboding, Tony studied the narrow treads. They were old and rotting and did not exactly invite you to climb up them! And what was more, it was even more dark and gloomy up there than it was down here! Perhaps he should just turn round and go back.

While he was thinking all this, he heard a low giggle. Then a clear voice called: 'Hello, Tony!'

Startled, he looked upwards, but could not see anybody.

'Where are you?' he called.

'Come and find us!' answered the voice.

'Or are you scared?' added a second.

'Scared? Not me!' lied Tony.

Weak at the knees, he climbed up the wooden steps. With each step, the treads creaked as if they might collapse at any moment. But at last he reached the top in safety.

He looked around uneasily. Everywhere there were piles of straw bales. There were so many, and among them so many hiding places, that he really did not know where to begin looking.

But then he had an idea. Quietly, so as not to give himself away, he went to a little hollow in the straw, crept inside – and waited. It surely would not be long before Jeremy and Joanna came out of their hiding places because they would be wondering where he was!

And he was right. After a while, he heard some excited whispers and someone slipped over the mounds of straw and came and stood quite close to Tony.

'Can you see him?' asked a voice.

'No.'

21

'Did he go back down again?'

'Dunno.'

Tony leaned forward till he could see a pair of yellow boots, blue trousers, a blue pullover and short, light hair. It was Jeremy.

Tony gave a surreptitious smile.

'Perhaps he's hiding?' said Jeremy.

'Shall we look for him?' asked Joanna.

'Yes. Come on.'

There was a cracking and rustling, steps ran here and there, and then Joanna's head emerged from among the straw bales.

'I've got him!' She pushed the straw aside. 'That was quite a trick! Just to wait till we came out ourselves!'

Tony was pleased he had managed to outwit them.

'You weren't expecting that!' he said, and stood up. As he brushed his pullover down, he gave Joanna a sideways look. In her jeans, red boots and with her fair hair tied back at her neck, she did actually look quite nice. When she noticed his interest, she went quite red.

'We'd found such a good place to hide,' she said hurriedly. 'Behind a wooden case.'

Tony gave a start. He hoped it was not the Little Vampire's coffin!

'Where is it?'

She pointed to a case near the wall. 'Over there. Behind our gran's trunk.'

The huge case with its old-fashioned lock was certainly not Rudolph's coffin. But perhaps he would be able to find out whether they knew anything about the vampire's

22

coffin. So he asked: 'Are there any other wooden boxes?'

'Why do you ask?' wondered Jeremy.

'Because –' Now what should he say? Since he could not think up any satisfactory reason, he said, 'Oh, I just wondered.'

'Just wondered!' mimicked Jeremy. 'I suppose you're some sort of treasure hunter?'

'Why don't you tell him that you've got another box?' asked Joanna, giggling.

Jeremy threw his sister a furious look. 'It's got nothing to do with Tony. Nor with you either!'

'What sort of box?' asked Tony anxiously.

'A box for his rubber monsters.'

'Rubber monsters?'

'Those flabby things made of rubber. Mum wanted to chuck them out, but he hid them up here.'

'So?' growled Jeremy. It was obvious he did not like talking about it, for he changed the subject quickly.

'Do you play table tennis?'

'Not very well,' said Tony.

'Jeremy can't either,' said Joanna. 'But I'm quite good.'

'Ha, ha!' said Jeremy and went over to the steps.

'I'm better than you!' cried Joannna.

Tony climbed down the steps behind Jeremy. On one hand, he was relieved and glad that the vampire had not hidden his coffin in the barn – on the other hand, now he still did not know where he was going to meet up with Rudolph that evening.

24

8

Weird Occupants

Tony had just won a table tennis game against Jeremy when Mrs Herring called them to supper.

'Shall we go to my room and play for a bit afterwards?' asked Jeremy. 'I'll give you a couple of my knights.'

'Let's wait and see,' Tony said evasively. 'I might go to bed,' he added with a yawn, although he was not at all tired.

'This early?'

'Well yes. It's the country air . . .!'

Jeremy looked disappointed. 'What a wally!'

Normally Tony would not have let a remark like that pass, but this time he just smiled.

'Then I'll just have to play with Joanna,' said Jeremy crossly. That suited Tony perfectly. Then he would be able to look for the coffin in peace. He might even find it before the Little Vampire flew off!

But Rudolph Sackville-Bagg had apparently hidden his coffin extremely well. Tony could find no trace of it anywhere when he looked round the yard after supper.

Finally, he came to a halt in front of a low building. It had no windows and looked like a garage. Cautiously Tony opened the iron door – and leapt backwards, for in the same instant the most deafening shrieks and cries broke out. Terrified, he slammed the door and raced back to the house. Not until he had reached the front door did he dare turn round for the first time. He was surprised to find no terrible monster was on his heels. Still shaking, he climbed the stairs to his room. He sat down on his bed and tried to think. Were they – animals? But what kind of animal lived in total darkness and made such a fearful racket?

He wondered whether the Little Vampire had anything to do with it. But a vampire would never make such a row; vampires acted silently and surreptitiously.

And then a terrible thought occurred to him. Suppose the Little Vampire had opened that same door in his search for a hiding place for his coffin, and the terrible creature inside had grabbed him and pulled him in . . . perhaps he was in there now, waiting in the vain hope that Tony would come and rescue him?

Tony decided to go downstairs and ask Joanna what exactly the low building was with its weird occupants.

Joanna was in the lounge watching television – a wildlife film, Tony noticed, feeling superior.

'I must ask you something,' he said.

'Not now,' she replied. 'Wait till the film's over.'

Tony groaned softly. The film would be bound to go on for another half hour, and that might be too long if he was going to be in time to help the vampire.

'But I absolutely have to know what's in the

low building,' he said urgently. 'Just now, when I opened the door –'

'You opened the door?' Joanna gave a low chuckle. 'I can just imagine what happened!'

'What's inside?'

'Didn't you know?' she giggled. 'Didn't you hear the squealing?'

'Squealing?' Suddenly he began to understand. 'Were they pigs then?'

'Yes,'

Tony realised he was going red. He'd been scared of pigs! But then it occurred to him that something still was not quite right: pigsties did not look like that! And pigs did not live in the dark?'

'I don't believe you!' he said boldly. 'Pigsties have windows!'

'But it isn't a normal pigsty,' explained Joanna. 'We keep pigs for fattening.'

'And they live in the dark?'

'Yes. They only see daylight when Dad goes to let their food in. That's why they make such a noise.'

'But that's animal torture!' said Tony, enraged.

Joanna shrugged her shoulders. 'At least my father doesn't have to clean them out anymore. Everything happens automatically.'

'It's still torture!'

'They weren't much better off in the old pigsty. You can take a look if you like. In any case, it's full of junk now.'

Tony pricked up his ears. An old pigsty full of junk? Perhaps the Little Vampire had chosen that as his hiding place?'

'Where exactly is it?'

'Behind the cowsheds – there, and now I want to watch my film, thank you!'

'I'm off now,' said Tony gratefully.

He was very pleased with all he had managed to find out.

9

Vampire Teeth

In the meantime, it had got dark outside. It was never as dark as this at home in the city, thought Tony with a shudder! The moon had vanished behind some clouds, and the light from the street lamps glimmered only faintly through the tall trees at the edge of the road. His torch would have come in really useful right now! But typical him, he had forgotten it in all the upheaval of packing his case.

When he finally reached the back of the cowsheds, he took a deep breath, in spite of the unbelievable stink: for there behind the manure heap he could make out the roof of a shed. It must be the old pigsty!

As he came nearer, he saw that it was made of brick, with small windows and a wooden door. And the door . . . was half open . . . !

Tony stopped still. His heart was beating wildly. Wasn't that a light at the window? And wasn't that a strange shadow that slipped out around the door? He shivered. Suppose it wasn't the Little Vampire at all who lived in the old pigsty, but – Aunt Dorothy, for instance! Or some other vampire, one from round here . . . .

And in the silence round about him, he suddenly heard a noise: it was a clear, clicking sound, the sound of needle-sharp teeth biting together! Vampire teeth!

Involuntarily, Tony took a couple of steps backwards . . . and came to a halt with one boot stuck firmly in the sticky ground. 'Rats!' he whispered quietly through tight lips. No matter how he twisted and pulled, his boot would not budge! That would have to happen now, when over by the pigsty there might be a vampire lying in wait for him!

Rigid with fright, Tony saw a figure detach itself from the darkness of the doorway and silently and stealthily come up to him. Its full-length cloak swelled out around it, so that it looked like some gigantic black bat.

At that moment, the moon came out from behind the clouds and Tony found himself looking at the deathly pale face of the Little Vampire!

'Rudolph!' he cried, his voice quivering from relief and emotion.

'Hi, Tony!' said the vampire gloomily.

Tony noticed his red-rimmed eyes and large mouth, with its widely-spaced canine teeth, as sharp as needles. At the sight of those vampire teeth, a shiver ran down his spine . . . .

'I – I was coming to visit you,' he said quickly.

'Visit me?' The vampire laughed huskily. 'What a good idea! If only you knew how hungry I am!'

'I didn't mean it like that!'

'How did you mean it then?' The vampire took a step nearer Tony.

Tony would have liked to have retreated, but his boot was still firmly stuck in the mud.

Cold sweat broke out on his forehead. But on no account must the vampire realise how frightened he was.

'I just wanted to find out where you had put your coffin,' he said evenly.

'My coffin?' The vampire's face took on a distrustful look. 'Why?'

There was only one answer to that!

'We're friends, aren't we?' said Tony, putting all his powers of persuasion into the words.

The vampire tightened his lips and growled: 'Friends! But I'm so flipping hungry!' And he cast a lingering glance at Tony's neck.

'Didn't I help you bring that heavy coffin all the way here?' asked Tony.

'Yes,' growled the vampire.

'And I even paid for the train tickets out of my own pocket money!'

The vampire looked at Tony testily. 'You're making it all sound as if it were done for my benefit!'

'Wasn't it?' cried Tony.

'You wanted me to come, because otherwise it would have been so boring for you out here on a farm! That's how you persuaded me to come with you!'

Tony had to smile. That was quite true – but the vampire also had his own good reasons for leaving the family vault for a couple of days!

'And what about George the Boisterous?' he cried. 'Hadn't Greg invited him to the vault to stay? And didn't that mean you had to make yourself scarce?'

'We-ell,' drawled the vampire. 'But I'm sure I wouldn't have chosen to come to this lousy farm,' he added fiercely. 'There is absolutely nothing fit for me to eat here. Yesterday I was out on the prowl for half the night and all I could catch was a mouse!'

'You just haven't found your way about yet,' said Tony. 'I bet you don't even know where the bullocks are yet!'

'Bullocks . . . that's all I need!' said the vampire grumpily.

'And there are hens!' continued Tony. 'I can show you where the henhouse is! And I even know where there is a l –' He was going to say 'lamb', but he hesitated as he thought of the cuddly little white bundle.

'What's a l –?' spat the vampire.

But Tony had decided not to tell him about the lamb. 'Laying hens!'

'Laying hens!' echoed the vampire. 'Just shut up about all these animals, will you!'

Tony held his breath and gave another tug at his boot – and this time he managed to get it free. With a sigh of relief, he said, 'Can I have a quick look?'

'A quick look at what?' asked the vampire suspiciously.

'At the pigsty. Or haven't you made yourself at home in there?'

'Yes I have. But hurry up! If only you knew how starving I am!'

10

The Little Vampire's Hideout

Tony slipped through the door of the pigsty behind the Little Vampire. They came into the first part, which was stacked high with old furniture. By the wall stood a tall cupboard with a long looking-glass. In the light that came from the main pigsty, Tony could see his reflection; but where the vampire should have been, the mirror was empty!

He spun round – and there was the vampire, large as life, with his tousled hair hanging to his shoulders, and his bespattered cloak with its moth holes. Tony gulped. He knew very well that a vampire cannot have a reflection. But there was quite a difference between reading about it in a book and actually finding out it was true in real life. But then he almost smiled: after all, it was not any old vampire, it was Rudolph Sackville-Bagg, his best friend. There was no need to be scared of him – was there?

All the same, he felt rather uncertain as he followed the vampire into the main pigsty. It was a long room with waist-high brick partitions for the pigs. Everywhere there were planks of wood, boards, old doors, furniture, tools, rolls of wire and iron stakes. The thick layer of dust over everything showed that hardly anyone ever ventured inside. On top of all that, it stank unbelievably of pig manure

and rotting things. But it was just the right hide-out for the vampire.

His little black coffin, hidden in a corner between a worm-eaten commode and a large chest, would not have been noticeable at all in amongst all this clutter – except that there was a candle burning on the edge of it! Tony knew Rudolph needed the candle so that he could read for a little while when he woke up – vampire stories, of course!

'What a fantastic hiding-place!' he said approvingly.

The vampire gave a pleased smile. 'Yes, isn't it? How did you manage to find me?'

Tony made a sweeping gesture. 'First I looked for you in the barn, and in with the pigs they keep for fattening. Then Joanna told me about this old pigsty.'

'Joanna?' asked the vampire suspiciously. 'Who's she? Does she know anything?'

Tony cleared his throat in embarrassment. 'She lives here on the farm. But she has no idea you are here as well – and anyway, she doesn't believe in vampires,' he added, even though he did not know if it were true, 'so you are completely safe.'

That seemed to calm the vampire. He went over to his coffin, pulled out a hat and put it on. Tony bit his lips in order not to laugh out loud: it was the Tyrolean hat which he had lent the vampire for the train journey! With the hat on his head, its long feather whipping up and down with every movement, the Little Vampire really did look quite a sight!

But Rudolph evidently thought he looked very fine, for he was smiling self-consciously.

'Shall we go?' he said.

'Where?'

'You were going to show me where I could get something to eat!'

11

Hen's Eyes

Once outside the shed, the vampire asked:
'Right, now where are the bullocks?'

'The b-bullocks?' Tony himself did not know
exactly where the pasture with the bullocks
was. 'What about going to the henhouse first?'
He tried to draw the vampire along another
tack.

'Hens!' said the vampire dismissively.
'They're made of nothing but bones and
feathers. I'd never get full up on that!'

'But there are lots and lots of them,'
countered Tony.

'Grrr!' was all the vampire said.

'The bullocks are very fierce,' tried Tony.

'Fierce?' the Little Vampire did not sound
quite so sure of himself. 'Do you mean they
might do something to me?'

'Well –'

'Then – then I will go the the henhouse first
of all,' agreed the vampire hastily.

Tony grinned to himself. The Little Vampire
always acted as if he were incredibly courageous and unafraid, but in fact he was just as
easily scared as Tony!

Would he be frightened of the hens? Tony
had already made up his mind never to go into
the henrun again himself. He would stand by
the fence and watch them all tweaking at the
vampire's holey old stockings! At the thought

of the vampire, cloak flapping, running about among all those pecking beaks, Tony gave a soft laugh.

But his humour was short-lived, for in the henrun, there was not a hen to be seen.

'Where are all these hens of yours?' growled the vampire with obvious disappointment.

'Well – they, er,' Tony began. He had expected to find them clucking about in the henrun. 'They, er, must be asleep.'

'Where?' asked the vampire, grinding his teeth.

Of course, Tony could not admit that he hadn't the faintest idea. He pointed to the little house where the broody hens were. 'In there.'

'All of them?' asked the vampire in disbelief. 'I thought you said there were lots and lots of them?'

'Some of them go to roost in the trees.'

'Hens? In trees?'

'Why not? They're birds, aren't they?'

'We vampires may not know much about wildlife,' declared the vampire, 'but hens in trees – I've never heard of that before!'

Nor have I, Tony secretly had to agree with him. Out loud, he said: 'Can't you see their eyes?'

The vampire obviously did not know what a chicken's eye looked like, because he became very serious and his sharp eyes, which after all could see much better in the dark than Tony's, peered up into the tops of the trees.

'There is something up there,' he said. 'I can't see any eyes, but I can see a shadow moving.'

39

'A shadow moving?' cried Tony in alarm. After all, he had made it all up about hens roosting in trees! 'Is it an animal!' he asked anxiously.

'It might be a vampire!' said Rudolph with a broad grin.

'A v-vampire?' Tony's voice was shaking.

Rudolph gave him an amused sideways glance. 'Since when have you been afraid of vampires?'

'I – er – it might be Aunt Dorothy.'

'Aunt Dorothy is much fatter than that.'

'Or Sabina the Sinister?'

'My grandmother does not go around lurking in the tops of trees,' retorted the vampire haughtily. 'But it might be Anna.'

'Anna? Did she want to come too?'

'She just always wants to be where you are!'

Tony felt himself going red. 'Is it her?'

The vampire giggled.

'Lovesick old Anna perched high in a tree
    Twittering just like a starling.
Down on the ground her beloved gazed up
    Wished he were next to his darling!'

'Very funny!' said Tony furiously. To get his own back, he said: 'I bet it's McRookery!' He knew how frightened the vampires were of the Nightwatchman at the cemetery, who was constantly on their trail and had vowed to get rid of the lot of them. Rudolph's Uncle Theodore had already fallen victim to him.

But the Little Vampire was unruffled. 'And since when has McRookery been able to fly?'

Now Tony could see the creature for himself. Slowly and rather clumsily, it flew down from the tree to the henrun. As it perched on the wire-netting fence, and gave a harsh and piercing cry, he suddenly knew what it was . . . .

But it was too late to tell the Little Vampire, for in the same instant he had taken to his heels and fled.

'Oh well,' said Tony going back to the farmhouse, 'he annoyed me with that stupid rhyme, so I forgot to warn him about the peacock . . . .'

12

Country People

The next morning, Tony's parents insisted that he go with them on their walk, even though he did not in the least bit feel like it.

'Otherwise you'll just sit there in your room!' declared his mother.

'Or mooch around the farm getting bored,' added his father.

'Going for a walk isn't exactly mind-blowing!' retorted Tony.

'Oh, it is,' said Dad. 'You'll soon see, there's a whole collection of interesting things to look at.'

Tony pointed to a couple of bags of rubbish that were sitting by the side of the road. 'Like those, I suppose you mean?'

'You know perfectly well what your father meant,' said Mum.

Tony was silent, irritated. It was always them who had to decide what was good for him!

Sulkily, he followed along behind them and tried to pick up as little as possible of their conversation about farmhouses, leaded windows and farmhouse curtains – which was not at all easy, because each of them kept drawing the other's attention to such 'objects of interest' with great enthusiasm.

How like tourists! he thought disdainfully.

When they went into raptures over a three-foot high windmill standing in someone's front garden, and its owners looked curiously over at them, Tony felt himself go bright red.

'Can't you talk a bit more quietly?' he hissed.

But unconcerned his parents merely began to question the people about their house, the windmill, and any other 'objects of interest' to be found in Nether Bogsbottom. Tony crossed to the other side of the road and pretended they were nothing to do with him. When he had counted to 25, his parents came over to him.

'Country people are so open and friendly!' enthused his mother.

'– unlike Tony here,' added Dad with a glance at Tony's sullen expression.

'At home you don't go around chatting up every other person, that's all!' he growled. 'You're behaving like real tourists!'

His mother just laughed. 'And now, like real tourists, we're going to have a look at the church!'

'That's all I need!' said Tony.

Then it occurred to him that if there was a church, there must be a graveyard – and that thought made him feel better.

But it was a recent graveyard, as Tony soon discovered to his disappointment. Surrounded by a low stone wall, its paths were dead straight and tidily raked, and it had only a few bushes and trees. The gravestones stood in such immaculate rows, and the graves themselves were so carefully tended, it made him yawn. There were certainly no vampire graves in this cemetery – or were there? In the last row, he found this epitaph:

Buried deep
In timeless sleep
Lies our earthly core;
What we loved
Lives on above
And forever more.

But the grave was much too well cared for to be a vampire's grave! Vampire graves, as far as Tony knew, had ancient weathered gravestones and were overgrown with weeds.

'Well, have you discovered a vampire grave?' asked his father when they all met up in front of the church.

'Indeed I have!' said Tony, who was irritated by his father's condescending tone of voice. 'The whole cemetery is full of them. And there's a vampire running round with a shovel and a wheelbarrow, trying to dig himself a grave. If you hurry up, you'll see him. He's wearing a blue cap and smoking a pipe.'

'And to think I was under the impression vampires only came out at night,' remarked his father in an amused tone.

Tony threw him a grim look and growled, 'What a know-all you are!'

'Can't you both talk about something else?' put in his mother heatedly. 'What about those old houses, for instance?'

'The houses really are pretty,' agreed

Dad promptly. 'Just look at that one with a balcony . . .'

Here we go again! thought Tony, grumpily following along behind.

His bad mood did not lift until they stopped on the way back at a shop with a signboard saying 'Gertie Grapple's Groceries'. The shop did not look at all like a grocer's, thought Tony. Nothing was set out or on display in either window, which were simply half covered over with coloured paper.

'Some grocery store!' he grinned.

'They're always like this in the country,' said his mother. 'Come on, let's go in.'

'Yes, let's,' agreed Tony. If it was the village shop, it would surely have biscuits and chocolate. And all he had had to eat that day was half a roll. But they were hardly inside before Tony's mother, noticing a long shelf full of confectionery, said: 'But we're not buying anything like sweets!'

'Why not?'

'Because you didn't eat a proper breakfast.'

'How mean!' he growled. They even had his favourite kind of chocolate here – his mouth watered at the thought. 'After all, it's my teeth that are going to get holes in them!'

But his mother shook her head. 'No!'

'But I want something sweet,' Tony said obstinately.

'I'll give you a lollipop,' said the lady at the cash till.

Tony's mother opened her mouth to protest, but then said nothing. She probably did not want to seem rude. But Tony could tell from the furrows on her forehead that she was furious with the sales lady for interfering in the way she was dealing with her son.

He took the lollipop with a grin and quickly stuck it in his mouth. 'You were right,' he remarked to his mother, 'country people are really nice!' He wandered happily round the shop. You could buy almost anything, from broomsticks to liver sausage. He even found some books. But none of them interested him. His mother, on the other hand, enthused loudly over them.

'Look here a minute, Tony, what lovely books these are. Animal stories! Books about hobbies! Adventure stories! Fairytales! Myths . . . . Shall I buy one for you?'

'No thanks.'

'But then you could spend this afternoon reading.'

I can do that anyway, thought Tony. Out loud, he said: 'They're just for village kids.'

'What do you like reading then?' enquired the sales lady.

Just to annoy his mother, Tony answered: 'Vampire stories!'

To his surprise, the lady did not laugh at his reply, but came out from behind the till, climbed some steps and took a few books down from a shelf – books with black covers, he noticed happily.

'Here,' she said, handing Tony three books. 'Do you like these better?'

They were – vampire stories! Tony had read

two of them already, but the third, with the promising title, *Your Ruby-red Blood, Katharina*, was new to him.

He turned to his mother and asked: 'Will you buy this one for me?'

'Most certainly not!' she answered crossly.

'My children enjoyed those books very much,' said the sales lady.

'You see?' said Tony triumphantly. 'Country people know what's good for them!'

The sales lady looked flattered and smiled, but she did not offer to give him the book, which was what he had hoped would happen. So he had to pay for it out of his own money. But that wasn't so bad – now he had one more good book and, what was more, he now knew just how he was going to spend the afternoon!

13

The Little Vampire
and the Monsters

When Tony went into the old pigsty that
evening, the vampire was still in his coffin.
The candle was burning, but the vampire was
not reading as he usually did. He had pulled his
motheaten black blanket right up to his chin
and he looked at Tony with bloodshot eyes.

'Aren't you well?' asked Tony.

The vampire pulled the blanket down so
that Tony could see a scratch on his neck.

'I'm wounded!'

Tony nearly laughed out loud – he did not

think the scratch was really that bad!

With a look of great suffering, the vampire said: 'I'm sure I'm going to get blood poisoning. Greg had it once. He very nearly died of it!'

'But vampires are dead already,' remarked Tony.

The vampire threw him a furious look, as he always did when Tony caught him exaggerating.

'So what?' he hissed. 'We can still get blood poisoning!' He touched the scratch gingerly. 'Is it very deep?'

'No,' Tony reassured him.

'If only I could see it! I can't look at it in a mirror . . . have I got a red mark on my neck? Greg said, if you get blood poisoning, you get a red mark as well.'

Tony had to smile. The only mark the vampire had on his neck was a black one – and that was dirt! But he thought he had better not say that out loud. 'You look perfectly normal to me,' he declared. And he was right. The vampire looked just as pale and dishevelled as he always did. Only the rings under his eyes might have been a little darker than usual.

'Normal!' humphed the vampire. 'After a night like that, I couldn't possibly look normal!'

'What on earth happened?' asked Tony curiously. The vampire looked at him with glittering eyes. 'The farmyard is full of monsters!'

'Monsters?' Tony did his best to stay serious. He could well imagine what sort of monsters the vampire had bumped into! 'If you mean that thing that gave the awful cry –'

But before Tony could explain that it was only the peacock they had seen, the Little Vampire interrupted him. 'That was harmless!' he cried. 'But while I was crossing the field, a monster came charging up to me – it was a big as a house and it hit me!'

Tony quickly put his hand over his mouth. It must have been one of the horses! 'Is that how you got the scratch?'

'The what?' asked the vampire, looking hurt.

'The – er – the wound, on your neck,' Tony corrected himself. 'Did the monster do it to you?'

'No,' said the vampire in a sepulchral voice. 'Another monster came galloping up to me. So with my last ounce of strength I jumped into some bushes.'

'And so your neck got scratched on the thorns?'

The vampire closed his eyes, as if the memory caused him great pain. 'No,' he said slowly, 'there was a third monster in the bushes.'

Tony gulped in order not to laugh. 'Not another one?'

'Yes. It must have been lying in wait for me, because it immediately fell on me and bit me in the neck. I fainted.'

'How terrible!' said Tony. It was probably best if he pretended to believe this story of a monster in the bushes, though in fact, he was quite convinced the vampire had simply

scratched himself on the thorns! With studied seriousness, he said, 'Then it must have been a vampire.'

'What do you mean?'

'Because it bit you on the neck.'

The vampire looked indignant. 'Vampires don't bite each other. No, it was definitely a monster!'

Tony had to smile at the horror in the Little Vampire's voice as he said the word 'monster'. The only monster here on the farm was – the Little Vampire himself!

'But I'm soon going to find out what sort of monster it was!' With these words, the vampire stood up and climbed out of his coffin.

'Now?' asked Tony excitedly. To go with Rudolph on a monster hunt could be really exciting.

'No. First I need something to eat.'

As always at the thought of the vampire's eating habits, Tony gave a shudder. Even so, he asked bravely: 'Shall we go together?' He could always look away when the vampire was actually feeding. 'I'll be very quiet.'

The vampire shook his head. 'No. You'd only disturb me.'

'I wouldn't,' Tony assured him eagerly.

'Why are you so keen to come along?' asked the vampire reluctantly.

'Why?' Tony took a deep breath. 'If only you knew how bored I've been today. The whole day, all I've done is go for a walk, read, eat . . . .'

The vampire looked at Tony sympathetically.

'I'd been so looking forward to this evening,' continued Tony persuasively.

'And what if I need to fly?' growled the vampire.

Tony had been waiting for that question. With a beaming smile, he pulled out the second cloak from under his jersey. 'Here. I'd thought of that, naturally.'

This seemed to convince the vampire, for his mouth creased into a grin of acknowledgement.

'Okay then,' he said, 'you can come with me. But don't you try to get mixed up in my – er – affairs while we're out!'

'Of course not!' Tony was only too glad to agree. Once outside, he asked, 'Where's your hat, by the way?'

'It's gone,' said the vampire gloomily.

'Gone?' That startled Tony. He himself could not care less what happened to his Tyrolean hat, but his parents were another matter. 'How did that happen?'

'I lost it when the first monster appeared.'

'Then it must be still in the field,' said Tony in a relieved voice. 'Come on, we'll go and get it.'

The vampire gave a cry of horror. 'Go after those monsters on an empty stomach? Never!' And as if he were afraid Tony might convince him otherwise, he took off into the air.

'Wait!' called Tony.

He quickly put on the cloak, which smelt of musty, mouldering coffins. It was made of black material and was already quite worn out and full of moth holes. With a beating heart, Tony stretched out his arms and moved them cautiously up and down – and at once he began to float. He gave a few more vigorous movements – and away he flew.

Soon the farmyard below looked like a model in a toyshop. Tony thought of his parents, of Joanna and Jeremy, of Mrs Herring and her husband, all sitting in the farmhouse and who had no idea that here he was, flying through the night sky – and suddenly he had to laugh out loud.

'Have you gone bonkers?' hissed the vampire furiously. 'Do you want everyone to see us?'

'No one will hear us up here,' Tony said defensively.

'You think so?' spat the vampire venomously. 'And what if Aunt Dorothy just happened to be flying past?'

Tony started. 'Can you see her somewhere?'

'No. But you never know,' replied the vampire. 'Now hurry up – I'm about to die of hunger!'

14

What a Courageous Vampire!

'Where are we going?' asked Tony.

The vampire pointed to the dome of a church in the distance, which looked rather like an onion.

'To Onionton,' he said, and added, 'I hope there won't be any monsters there!'

I'm sure there won't be, thought Tony, but there will be people!

That afternoon, he had made up a song, and it seemed to be appropriate now. So as they flitted through the night together, he began to sing softly:

'When Rudolph reached a hundred years
  A present came from Grandma:
  A woollen cloak with magic power
  To help him fly and soar and tower –
  Now he was a true vampire!'

'What are you singing?' asked the vampire, ears suddenly pricked. 'Are you singing about me?'

Tony grinned. 'Maybe.'

'Sing it again!' demanded the vampire.

'Only if you promise not to get cross,' said Tony, and he began to sing, while the vampire listened attentively.

'When Rudolph reached a hundred years
  A present came from Grandma:

A woollen cloak with magic power
To help him fly and soar and tower –
Now he was a true vampire!

Out of the vault Rudolph did fly
And winged his way through the night sky.

The air was cold, and down below
A wood seemed just the place to go.

But in the wood he met a bear.
Poor Rudolph! That was quite a scare!

Back to the town he turned and flew
But Rudolph's luck was out there too.

A thousand street lamps burning bright
Made sure the town was full of light.

'Let's catch him quickly!' came the cry
As lots of people saw him fly.

They chased him round with nets and sticks.
Poor Rudolph was in quite a fix.

Frightened and scared, he found a hole –
He's still there now, for all I know!'

'Not bad!' said the vampire when Tony had
finished. 'But it's not quite true to life.'
'Why?' said Tony.
'Because no vampire would ever crawl into
a hole,' explained the Little Vampire. 'And
vampires aren't scared, either. I would sing

it like this:

> Brave Rudolph was no scaredy-cat –
> He bit them all, and that was that!'

He gave his raucous grating laugh.

Tony just clamped his mouth shut knowingly. They would soon see just how brave the vampire really was, because already the first houses of the little town were springing up below them.

With a grin, Tony pointed to a brightly lit house whose front door stood wide open. Several smartly dressed people were going inside.

'If you're so brave,' he said, 'there's just the chance to prove it!'

'What do you mean?'

'There seems to be some sort of party going on down there.'

'But I don't want to dance.'

'You don't have to dance!' Tony tried to stay serious. 'But just think of all those people. It's just the chance you've been waiting for!'

Now a taxi drew to a halt in front of the house and two men got out.

'You see?' said Tony. 'And there are more coming along the street. After all, you are very courageous,' he added sarcastically.

'I'm not tha-at courageous,' said the Little Vampire plaintively. In the face of so many people, he had gone even paler than usual. 'I would, er, rather find a more quiet spot,' he murmured, turned away and flew speedily off in another direction.

Tony followed him, singing half out loud:

'Courageous Rudolph found a hole –
He's still there now, for all I know!'

15

Seeing into the Future

At first, Tony thought the Little Vampire was going to fly back to the farm, for he took the same route as they had in coming here. But then he turned right at a sign, on which was written: West Batsteeple 2 miles. When a small thatched farmhouse came into view, he slowed down and turned to Tony. With a jerk of his head, he pointed to the farmhouse. It stood among tall trees. Above the blue front door, an old-fashioned lamp was burning, and two of the windows on the ground floor were lit up.

'Just the place for me!' said the vampire eagerly. 'I bet an old couple live there with six grandchildren. The children will already be asleep, and their grandparents will be about to join them – the children's parents were probably killed in a plane crash,' he added in a whisper.

Tony was amazed at the vampire's fertile imagination.

'In the stables they have cows and horses and lambs –' As he listed these animals, the vampire's voice took on such a longing, hungry note that Tony shuddered. 'They're bound to have locked the front door,' the vampire went on excitedly, 'old people are careful. But I bet they've forgotten to bolt the back door. Old people are forgetful, too.' He broke out into a grating laugh and landed in the shadow of a tall tree. 'Come on, Tony!'

'Wouldn't you rather go on alone? You said yourself I would only disturb you.'

'No. You know your way around houses better than me.'

'I don't know much about farmhouses.'

'You just want to get out of it!'

'I do not!' contradicted Tony.

'Well then,' grinned the vampire. 'Let's just go and see if the back door is open.'

Tony looked over at the house. With its bright curtains, window-boxes under the windows, and the blue front door, it really did not look so very forbidding – more as if kindly, harmless people lived there.

'Okay,' he said, 'if you go first.'

'Suits me,' grunted the vampire.

Slowly and carefully, he made his way towards the house and opened the little wrought iron gate which led to the garden.

'Come on!' he hissed to Tony.

Tony followed on tiptoe, but he could not manage to move as silently as the vampire between the shrubs and flower beds in the garden: again and again, twigs snapped and gravel crunched under his feet – or a bird he had not noticed would fly up in front of him with a start. At every sound, the vampire turned round and glared at him.

Luckily, no one in the house seemed aware of their presence, for the windows facing the garden remained in darkness.

At last, they came to a little terrace on which

stood a round table, four chairs and a barbecue.

'You go and see if the garden door is open!' commanded the vampire.

'Why me?' protested Tony.

'Because I've got better eyes and must stay on guard here,' replied the vampire – not very convincingly, Tony thought. Nevertheless, wobbly at the knees, he walked over to the door and hesitantly pushed the handle downwards. The door was locked!

The vampire cracked his fingers nervously. 'Then we'll have to try round the front,' he said, and added pompously, 'I expect the old dears have muddled up the doors. I bet they've forgotten to lock the front one.'

'You ought to take up seeing into the future!' Tony said cuttingly.

But instead of being offended, the vampire merely smiled. In a strangely lulling tone of voice, he said: 'Oh no, not me. You're the one who sees into the future!'

'What do you mean?' asked Tony suspiciously.

The vampire grinned. 'You must go to the front door, open it and see what the future holds in store for us!'

For a moment, Tony was speechless. Then he exclaimed hotly: 'That would suit you very well, wouldn't it! You're always sending me on ahead! And only because you're such a coward!'

'What did you call me? A coward?' The vampire's voice crackled with rage. 'That's the most shameful idea I've ever –'

He got no further, because at that moment, a light went on in the room facing the terrace. The door opened and a young woman in a long, green dress came out.

'So there you are at last!' she cried, and her voice sounded friendly and excited.

16

Two Visitors from Manchester

Tony and the Little Vampire were so taken
aback that they stood motionless as if struck
by lightning – even when a tall, broad-
shouldered man in a blue dressing-gown
appeared behind her.

'Our holiday children are here!' the woman
cried. 'It's Bernard and Roger from Manchester!'

'This is a surprise!' the man replied in a
rumbling voice. 'Did you miss your train?'

Tony thought quickly. Obviously the man
and the woman were expecting two children
from Manchester to spend their holidays with
them who, for some reason, had been delayed.
Now presumably they thought Tony and
Rudolph were these same children! This was a
stroke of luck for him and the Little Vampire.
All they had to do was to act as if they were the
children, and to wait for the first available
opportunity to scarper!

'We got on the wrong train by mistake!' he
said bravely.

'The wrong train?' asked the woman. 'But
didn't your mother see you off?'

'Yes,' said Tony, 'but she put us on the
wrong one.' He added with a grin, 'You see,
she didn't have her glasses on!'

The woman shook her head in disbelief.

'When did you first notice?'

'What? That she didn't have her glasses on?'

'That you were on the wrong train!'

Before Tony could think of an answer to this, the man said, 'That doesn't matter now. We're very pleased you've got here at last, and hope that these four weeks' holiday will do you good.'

'Four weeks!' cried the vampire in horror.

The man laughed. 'I don't think four weeks will be long enough for you, you look so pale!'

'My friend needs a bit of time to get used to country air,' said Tony quickly. 'He's a real towny, you see.'

'Your friend?' said the woman in surprise. 'But the letters from the Youth Welfare Office said you were brothers!'

'Half-brothers,' said Tony.

He had the feeling that the whole thing was becoming rather risky. What was more, the Little Vampire had a look on his face as if he was about to take to his heels, and if he did that, everything would be ruined, because the man and the woman would be bound to be suspicious. And what might happen after that, Tony preferred not to think about!

He said quickly: 'We must go and fetch our luggage. Come on, Roger.'

The vampire looked at Tony blankly. 'What luggage?' he grumbled.

Tony tried to stay calm, even though his heart was beating furiously. 'Our cases? You know!' As he spoke, he looked entreatingly at the vampire. At last the penny seemed to have dropped.

'Oh yes,' he nodded, 'our cases.'

Tony gave a sigh of relief.

'Your cases?' repeated the man in astonishment. 'Aren't they in the luggage office?'

'They – they're back there,' said Tony, pointing in the direction they had come from. 'We left them on our way here. Come on, Roger!' he urged the vampire.

'Just a moment,' said the man, 'I'll come with you, of course. Just let me go and change into something else.' With that, he went into the house.

Tony held his breath. This was the moment he had been waiting for.

'We'll go on ahead,' he said to the woman. Then he beckoned to the vampire and they disappeared into the bushes and shrubs. Once out of sight, they spread their cloaks and flew.

Once aloft, the whole adventure seemed quite funny to Tony, and he said: 'Tomorrow it'll say in the *West Batsteeple Gazette*: "Two boys from Manchester disappear into thin air! There is a suspicion they have been eaten!" '

But the vampire was not in the mood for jokes. With a grim look on his face, he flew to the sign which said: West Batsteeple 2 miles. There, he declared: 'From now on, I'll go on alone.'

'Why?' asked Tony in surprise.

'With you around, all I've had is bad luck!' said the vampire.

'I beg your pardon!' Tony was outraged.

'You seem to have forgotten that I just about saved your life!'

'Pah –!' The vampire snorted contemptuously. 'You were the one who lured me to that farm in the first place!'

'I lured you?' said Tony flabbergasted. 'And who said: "That looks just the place for me"?'

In his most ghostly voice, the vampire said: 'You did.'

'Me?' Tony was speechless.

'Yes, you!' exclaimed the vampire. 'If you hadn't spun me that tale about old people who always forget to lock their back doors, I would have flown on!'

Tony gasped for air. 'You always manage to put the blame on someone else!' he yelled. 'You – you – egoist!!'

The vampire's face lit up. 'Egoist? Now that sounds good. Is it something wicked?'

Tony did not reply.

'It must be something wicked,' said the vampire happily. 'Just wait till I tell Greg and Aunt Dorothy that someone called me an egoist!'

'Then you can also tell them at the same time that you are the meanest, most unreliable so-and-so I have ever met!' cried Tony. 'And I don't want to have any more to do with you!'

He turned sharply in the air. As he flew away, he could see the vampire still crouching on the signpost, with a self-satisfied smile on his face.

17

Vampires? No Thanks!

Tony spent the following morning in bed. He told his parents he had a tummy ache. It was not actually true, but after his row with the vampire and the lonely flight home, he had to have a little rest.

He took *Vampire Stories for Advanced Readers* out of the cupboard, where he had hidden it under his pullover, and turned to one of his favourite stories: *The Bats* by David Grant. It was about a boy who kept bats in an old shed. He was trying to tame them. And two little puncture marks on his neck betrayed how he managed to do it . . . .

Whenever Tony had read this story in the past, a pleasant shudder had come over him. But today he felt a sudden violent dislike of bats, which even took himself by surprise. Did it have something to do with his anger with the Little Vampire?

Crossly, he snapped the book shut and put it back in the cupboard. Then he had a look at the titles of the books which stood on the little shelf above Joanna's bed. *My Pony and Me*, *Adventures at the Stableyard*, *The Old Man and the Pony*, *The Golden Pony Book*. After a short hesitation, he took out *Adventures at the Stableyard*. On the back cover, it said it was a story about the theft of a pony. He lay down on his bed again and began to read.

That afternoon, when he met Joanna and Jeremy in front of the barn, he said to Joanna: 'You know, your books aren't too bad!'

'Do you think so?' She was pleased.

'*Adventures at the Stableyard* is really very exciting.'

'I thought you were only interested in vampire books.'

Tony made a dismissive gesture. 'Vampires? No thanks!' he declared, so loudly that even the Little Vampire in his coffin might have heard him.

'But haven't you got a friend who's a vampire?'

'Who told you that?'

'Our mum.'

'How's she supposed to know?' asked Tony scornfully.

'Isn't it true?' asked Jeremy nosily.

'Do you believe in vampires?' replied Tony.

'No.'

'Well then.'

Joanna was more obstinate. 'Have you got a friend who's a vampire, or not?'

'I haven't got a *friend* who's a vampire,' answered Tony, and that was completely truthful, for Rudolph Sackville-Bagg might be a vampire, but he was certainly not his friend any more!

'If you don't want any more to do with vampires, we could play with my knights if you like,' suggested Jeremy.

And why not? thought Tony. Playing with knights might not be as boring as he had thought. What was more, he had firmly decided to keep out of the Little Vampire's way in future – he was so conceited, smug and ungrateful! Rudolph Sackville-Bagg could just wait and see how he got on without him!

'All right,' said Tony, 'and after supper we could play together too,' he added, 'I've got nothing else in particular to do.'

18

Funny Business with the Eggs

The next morning, Tony was the first one
down to the breakfast table.

'So you're up already?' said his father in
astonishment, when he came down ten
minutes later.

'Well, yes,' said Tony, embarrassed. 'It does
sometimes happen.'

Naturally, he was not going to let on to his
father that he had quarrelled with the Little
Vampire and had therefore gone to bed at nine
o'clock, after having spent two boring hours
with Jeremy and his knights. Knights just
weren't the same as vampires!

'Isn't Mum awake yet?' he asked.

'No. She hardly slept a wink last night.'

At that moment, the two ladies who were
also guests at the farmhouse came in. Up till
now, Tony had prudently avoided meeting
them, because the two ladies had travelled on
the same train as himself and the Little
Vampire. He peered anxiously over at them,
but they took not the slightest notice of him.

The smaller of the two turned to Tony's
father and said excitedly: 'Couldn't your wife
sleep either? We've been here since Saturday
and haven't had a proper night's sleep yet!'

'Because of all the noises,' added the larger
lady.

'What sort of noises?' asked Tony's father.

'Terrible cries! As if someone was being strangled!' answered the larger lady.

'And then there are those giant moths fluttering around the house,' continued the smaller one. 'Yesterday, when we couldn't sleep, we were going to open a window, and there we saw a moth as big as a child! It was squatting on the window-sill staring at us. Ah, I won't forget those horrible red eyes as long as I live!'

Tony's father smiled benignly. 'What a pity my son didn't see it.'

'Why?' cried Tony, indignant that his father should have directed the ladies' attention to him.

'Well, it sounds like a vampire, doesn't it?'

The two ladies exchanged looks.

'Are there vampires round here?' asked the smaller one.

'Of course!' said Dad. 'These old sheds and stables are just up their street!'

Tony looked at his father in alarm. Did he know something about the Little Vampire's hiding place? However, his father's jovial expression showed he had only been joking.

'There certainly are not any vampires!' Tony declared.

His father looked surprised. 'What about your friend?'

'What friend?'

'Your friend Rudolph Deathbed-Wagg.'

'He is not my friend!' said Tony irritably. Just now, everyone seemed to be asking him about Rudolph Sackville-Bagg!

'Friend or not – haven't you always said he was a vampire?' asked Dad.

Luckily, at that very moment, Mrs Herring came in with the breakfast tray, so Tony was spared a reply. She put down the tray on the table and said: 'I'm sorry, but this morning I can't offer you any eggs. Someone has been in with the hens and has punctured all the eggs.'

'Who would have done that?' exclaimed Tony's father heatedly.

'I wish I knew,' she replied, looking enquiringly at Tony. But he remained unmoved – after all, he was innocent!

'It was probably a kid's prank,' she went on, 'but a very unfunny one, to my mind!'

The emphasis on 'kid' made Tony cross.

'It could just have well been a grown-up!' he retorted.

'Oh yes?' said Mrs Herring doubtfully. 'Do you really believe a grown-up would hit upon the idea of making little holes in all the eggs and sucking them dry?' She took a little brown egg out of her jacket pocket and held it out to Tony's father. 'Here, take a look at this!'

'It's completely empty!' he said, shaking his head.

Tony did his best to look unmoved, but he was itching to examine the two holes in the egg more closely: they were about as big as the point of a pencil and about an inch apart.

'Perhaps it was a tramp?' suggested the smaller of the two ladies.

'Or a fox?' said the larger.

'A fox with two legs!' said Mrs Herring,

73

eyeing Tony. He felt himself colour under her searching gaze. Now she was bound to think it had been him! But he always went red when anyone stared hard at him!

'I – I had nothing to do with it!' he cried hastily. 'I was in bed by nine o'clock!'

Mrs Herring only smiled disbelievingly. 'We'll probably never find out who it really was,' she said. 'But I only hope whoever it was is too sensible to try it again. Next time, he won't get away with it so easily!'

'Why do you say 'he'?' protested Tony. 'It could equally well have been a girl or a lady!'

But the subject was closed as far as Mrs Herring was concerned. 'You understand quite well what I mean,' she said shortly. Then she laid the table and went back to the kitchen.

'That was a pretty stupid idea of yours,' said Dad when she had gone.

'What was?' Tony did not understand.

'That business with the eggs.'

'But it wasn't me!'

Tony's father said evenly: 'I would like you to go to Mrs Herring, now, and apologise.'

'What?' Tony gasped. 'I've got to apologise, even though I haven't done anything?' He jumped up. 'You can find yourself another scapegoat!' he cried, and ran out.

Once in his room, he threw himself on his bed in a temper. How mean can you get? he thought. He had protested his innocence loud and clear. But grown-ups were pig-headed and always had to be right – and they were stupid! You only had to look closely to see that the two holes were the marks of a vampire's bite! If Tony wanted, he could show them who had made the holes in the eggs. He had only to take them to the old pigsty . . . .

No! He would never do that! When all was said and done, the Little Vampire had been his best friend – and perhaps he still was? Tony realised that his anger at Rudolph Sackville-Bagg had almost evaporated. Now he was far more angry about the cheek of his father and Mrs Herring in trying to lay the blame at his feet.

That evening, he decided, he would go and find the Little Vampire and make it up with him – and advise him to give the henhouse a wide berth in future! Suddenly he felt like finishing the story about the bats.

19

Something Must Be Done About Boredom

It was shortly before lunchtime and Tony was just practising turns on the upright bar when he saw his mother come out of the house. She came towards him with such determined strides that he quickly pulled himself up on top of the bar.

She came to a halt in front of him.

'Will you come down here a moment?' she said.

'Why?'

'I want a word with you.'

'If I must . . .' he said, pretending to be cool. His father and Mrs Herring were bound to have told her about the eggs that had been sucked dry and now, as his mother, she was going to have a go at wringing a confession from him. But she wasn't going to have any luck! With deliberate slowness, Tony slid off the iron bar.

'What did you want to discuss?' he asked innocently.

'Dad's told me everything,' she began.

That did not surprise Tony in the least.

'So, we've been thinking . . . it was us who persuaded you to come on this trip . . . .' Persuaded? Forced, more like it, thought Tony.

' . . . and perhaps you really are too old for a

holiday on a farm.' She paused. 'And so you're getting bored and that's why you come up with these crazy ideas.'

'What?' exclaimed Tony indignantly. 'What crazy ideas are you talking about?'

'You know quite well what I mean,' she answered evasively.

'I do not!' he said vehemently, although of course he did know what she was referring to. But for Pete's sake, he had nothing to do with it! 'If you think it was me who broke the eggs, you're quite wrong.'

But his mother just smiled. Apparently she had decided tactfully to leave the subject alone.

'And something must be done about boredom,' she went on steadily. 'That's why we've decided to take you on a night-time stroll this evening.'

She looked at him eagerly and seemed to expect him to be pleased. Normally he would have been – but not today!

'Couldn't we go for one tomorrow?'

'No. Tomorrow Dad and I want to take you on a paperchase.'

Oh no! groaned Tony softly. If only he could think up some excuse! 'My – my leg hurts!'

'All of a sudden?'

'Yes, I twisted it.'

'I see. But I'm sure your leg will be better by this evening. We won't set off till after supper.'

'Couldn't we at least go before supper?'

'Why should we do that?'

'Well, it won't be so dark then.' Even Tony realised how ridiculous that sounded, especially coming from him – he was the one who revelled in vampires, horror stories and grisly films!

His mother merely gave him a mocking glance. Then she turned round and went back to the house.

'Well, I can only go for half an hour!' Tony called after her. 'At the very most!'

But naturally the night-time stroll lasted much longer. They did not get back to the farm until half past ten! Tony was totally worn out: three times they had lost their way and finally, in an attempt to jump over a little stream, he had fallen in the cold water. After all that, both his legs were hurting!

He took off his soaking wet trainers in the boiler room next to the kitchen. His jeans were also wet through up to his hips, so he hung them on a line.

'You look about as cheerful as a month of wet Sundays!' teased his father.

'My throat hurts!' groaned Tony. He really did have a tickle in his throat.

'Have you caught a chill?' enquired his mother.

'Bound to have,' he said in secret malicious glee. Let them worry about him! After all, this stupid night-time stroll had been their idea!

'Then you must quickly have a cup of hot milk and honey. I hope Mrs Herring is still awake.'

'There's a light on in the lounge,' said Tony, giving a loud, painful-sounding cough.

His mother jumped. 'Go and quickly hop into bed.'

'What about my milk?'

'I'll bring it to you.'

Tony grinned contentedly. He liked hot milk and honey, especially in bed! But this time he had to wait an unusually long time for it. He had almost fallen asleep when his mother finally bought in a large glass of milk. Cautiously he took a sip.

'But this is cold!' he exclaimed indignantly.

'Oh? Is it?'

'Yes. Normally it's so hot I can hardly drink it.'

'Then it must have cooled down,' said his mother.

'Mrs Herring had so much to tell me, you see.'

Tony pricked up his ears. 'What about?'

'Someone's been in the henrun again and sucked all the eggs dry.'

Tony jumped. 'Did Mrs Herring see him?'

'Who?'

'The . . .' 'Little Vampire' was on the tip of Tony's tongue. 'The . . . thief.'

'No. When Mrs Herring went to the henhouse at about ten o'clock, it had already happened. And all the eggs have the same little holes as yesterday.'

'So now you can't suspect me any more!' cried Tony.

'No, it can't have been you,' said his mother

with a smile – rather an embarrassed one, Tony was pleased to notice. 'But soon we will know who's wreaking havoc in the henhouse!' she declared.

'How?'

'Mrs Herring has told a neighbour. He's coming tomorrow and bringing his dog with him.'

'Oh no!' Tony couldn't stop himself. Poor Rudolph Sackville-Bagg!

'Why does that upset you?' asked his mother. 'Are you scared of dogs suddenly?'

'Not of dogs,' said Tony. 'But I am of neighbours!'

20

The Butterfly Collector

Tony found out just how right he was the next
afternoon, when he bumped into Joanna in the
yard.

'Who is this neighbour of yours who's
coming this evening?' he asked.

'Oh him,' said Joanna lightly. 'He's our old
village doctor.'

Tony gave a sigh of relief – but only for a
moment, because she went on, 'Actually he's
interested in the same hobby as you!'

'What's that?' he asked suspiciously.

She giggled. 'Vampires!'

Tony gave a start.

'He's called Dr Rummage,' she continued
easily. 'Dr Ernest Albert Rummage. The name
suits him because he's always rummaging
around.' She laughed, but Tony was not in the
mood for a joke.

'What did you mean about vampires?' he
asked.

'You ought to take a look in his house!' said
Joanna. 'He has all the books there are about
vampires and bats. And in his livingroom
there is a glass cupboard – and I bet you can't
guess what's inside it!'

'I dunno,' said Tony, who already sus-
pected that whatever Dr Rummage kept
in his glass cupboard, it was nothing very
nice.

Joanna explained in a whisper: 'Impaled moths!'

'Impaled moths?' repeated Tony, shocked.

'Yes. Just imagine, he sticks a pointed matchstick through their bodies!'

Tony gulped. 'Are the moths – er – big?'

'No. They're just butterflies.'

'I see,' said Tony in relief. For a moment he had been afraid they might be impaled baby vampires! Even so, Dr Rummage sounded a more and more unpleasant character. And the situation was really becoming quite grave for Rudolph Sackville-Bagg! 'Do you know when he's due to come?'

'After supper,' said Joanna.

21

Dr Rummage

There were chips for supper, but Tony hardly managed to eat a mouthful. He fidgeted about on his chair and kept looking outside. When a car drove into the yard and pulled up, his heart was in his mouth. But it was only Mr Herring.

'I think you must have a temperature,' remarked his mother, who had been watching him.

'Oh no, I don't think so,' he was quick to reassure her. On no account must she think he was ill, otherwise she would send him to bed!

'What about your throat hurting?' she asked.

'It's better,' he lied.

'Is it?' she asked doubtfully. 'Your eyes look very bright and feverish.'

'I feel terrific!' he assured her.

Perhaps she was right after all. Perhaps he was ill. But at the moment, it did not matter. Only one thing was important now: he had to warn the Little Vampire before Dr Rummage appeared with his dog!

'May I go out?' he asked, trying not to let his parents see how nervous he was.

'Don't you really want any more to eat?' asked his mother.

'I'll . . . I'll take an apple with me!' replied Tony quickly. He could always be sure of getting on the right side of his parents with fruit and vegetables! It seemed to work this time as well, for his mother said more gently: 'All right then. But when it starts to get dark, come straight back indoors.'

'Okay,' he promised, thinking to himself that in any case, once it was really dark outside, he would not be able to achieve anything, because by then the vampire would have flown off into the night. No, Tony would have to catch him while he was still in his coffin.

As he went out of the front door, a small black van was just turning into the drive. It looks more like a hearse! thought Tony, and stood still in fright. A man in a dark coloured jacket got out. It had to be Dr Rummage! He was of medium height and had grey hair combed back from his forehead. His prominent black eyebrows and long hooked nose gave his a face dark and menacing expression, or so Tony thought, and he could not help taking a step or two backwards. But Dr Rummage paid no attention to him. He went to the back of his van and opened it. An enormous black dog jumped out.

Tony stood as if rooted to the spot, and stared at the dog. It was the size of a mastiff, but its coat was long and shaggy. All you could see of its face were its teeth, and they were so large and pointed that they gave Tony goose-pimples.

The dog must have been well-trained, because when its master said: 'Heel!' it trotted by his side without a lead over to the door. As he went past, Dr Rummage glanced at Tony, nodded shortly to him, and then disappeared into the house. After the door had closed behind him and the dog, Tony took a deep breath. That dog wasn't a dog – it was a monster!

Luckily the monster was now in the house. And Dr Rummage would surely spend a couple of minutes chatting with Mrs Herring. . . . And that short space of time would have to do for Tony to convince the Little Vampire that he must not stay one moment longer on the farm!

'I do hope the vampire is awake, at least!' thought Tony, as he raced round the barn to the old pigsty.

22

A Visit from a Lady

Tony cautiously pushed up the rusty old catch which held the pigsty closed. It was a catch that could be opened from the outside or the inside. Slowly, and with a squeak, the door opened . . . . The strong smell of decay that hit him told Tony that the Little Vampire was still at home. And he must be awake, for a feeble light came from the further partition.

Tony shut the door behind him and called: 'Rudolph! It's me, Tony!'

The only answer was a bright giggle.

Tony hesitated. Did that sound like the Little Vampire?

'Rudolph!' he called again. 'It's me!'

'Come on in!' said a croaky voice – the voice of the Little Vampire.

'Are you alone?' asked Tony uneasily.

Again he heard the bright giggle. Then the Little Vampire said: 'There's a lady waiting for you.'

'A lady?' repeated Tony, startled. 'Not – Aunt Dorothy?'

'Come and see for yourself!' answered the Little Vampire with a grating laugh. The fact that he was laughing reassured Tony. It definitely could not be Aunt Dorothy!

'Is it Anna?' he asked in a husky voice.

A fresh bout of giggles was the reply. So it was Anna! Tony let out his breath, and with

beating heart, went into the stall.

Anna was sitting at the foot of the coffin. Her little round face seemed to glow in the candlelight. She looked at him so adoringly with her huge eyes that he went quite hot.

'Good evening, Tony!' she said with a smile.

'Hallo Anna!' he replied, going red.

'I just had to see you,' she said, and went red too.

'M-me?' Tony couldn't think of a better reply.

'You didn't think she was missing *me*?' croaked the vampire from the coffin.

'I brought something with me,' said Anna, and took a red book from under her cloak. 'My autograph book.' She showed it to him proudly. 'You can be the first human to write in it!'

'There's already a poem by me in it!' announced the Little Vampire. 'Do you want to hear it?' And without waiting for an answer, he recited in a smug voice:

'If you give me blood
I feel very good.
But wine on the chill
Makes me feel quite ill.'

Anna looked at him sideways and said bitingly: 'If I were you, I wouldn't draw attention to that!'

'And why not?' asked the Little Vampire with a glitter in his eyes.

'Because it isn't a proper poem. "Blood" and "good" don't rhyme.'

'So what?' growled the vampire. '"Chill" and "ill" do!'

'In a proper poem, all the lines have to rhyme,' Anna contradicted him.

The vampire shrugged his shoulders. 'Then I'll simply recite it like this,' he said, making 'blood' rhyme with 'good':

'If you give me blood
I feel very good.
But wine on the chill
Makes me feel quite ill.'

'Eeugh!' said Anna contemptuously. 'That's very bad English!' The Little Vampire looked hurt, shut his mouth and was silent.

'Will you write something for me in here?' said Anna to Tony, looking at him entreatingly.

But Tony did not reply. He had suddenly gone deathly white.

'What's up?' she asked.

'There's someone outside!' he said in a shaky voice.

The Little Vampire gave a start of alarm. 'Outside the pigsty?'

'Yes. And I know who it is: Dr Rummage! He's come here this evening especially because he wants to find out who keeps sucking the eggs dry in the hen-house.'

'Why are you only telling us all this now?' cried the vampire.

'Because –' began Tony, then stopped. Should he admit that Anna had completly confused him? That when she looked at him with those big eyes, he forgot everything else?

But the vampire did not seem to want to wait for an answer. He leapt out of his coffin and called to his sister: 'We must fly!'

'But you won't get very far!' protested Tony gloomily. 'Dr Rummage has a dog, a real monster, as big as a calf.'

'Then we must barricade the door!' cried the vampire, tugging at the large chest which lay by his coffin. 'Help me!'

Anna did not move. Gently she said: 'I've got a much better idea – if Tony will go along with it,' she added with a fervent look at Tony.

'What sort of idea?' asked Tony suspiciously.

'You must go outside and talk to this Dr Rummage.'

'Me?' cried Tony. 'But I –' I'm scared of him too! was what he wanted to say, but then he thought differently, because he did not want to look stupid. Instead he asked cautiously: 'What shall I go and talk to him about?'

'That doesn't matter. You just get him away from here.'

Tony hesitated. It wasn't a bad idea – and probably the only means of escape for the vampires. Even so . . . . 'It's always me who has to do everything,' he grumbled.

Anna smiled sweetly at him. 'That's because you're a human! And you humans have a far easier time of it in almost everything than we do!'

'You can say that again,' agreed the vampire.

Tony sighed, resigned to his fate, 'Okay,' he said, 'I'll go.'

23

The Mysterious Man

Tony had hardly closed the pigsty door behind
him when something black came bounding up
to him; at a command from behind, it sat down
just a couple of strides from him. It was Dr
Rummage's dog! Tony did not dare move. He
had the feeling that the monster would tear
him to bits if he so much as twiched his little
finger! When Dr Rummage appeared, he was
quite relieved.

'What are you doing here?' asked Dr
Rummage.

'I – I was looking for something,' murmured
Tony.

'What?'

'A – er – a piece of paper with a telephone
number.'

'And you lost it just here?'

'Well, somewhere round here –'

'You've already looked in that shed?' Dr
Rummage pointed to the old pigsty. 'In fact, I
did hear you searching in there.'

Tony tried to keep calm. 'That's right,' he
said, 'but the piece of paper wasn't there.'

'Did anything in the shed strike you as
suspicious?'

'Suspicious? No, not at all,' Tony reassured
him.

Dr Rummage looked irresolutely over at the
pigsty. 'I was just about to investigate what

was going on in that shed,' he declared. 'But if you're sure you noticed nothing suspicious . . . there's a lot of old junk in there, isn't there?'

'Yes. Just a lot of junk.'

'Then I can spare myself a look.'

'You can indeed!' Tony agreed, trying to keep back a smile.

'Tell me something, have you any idea who keeps sucking the eggs dry?' Dr Rummage's voice took on a confidential note, almost friendly. Obviously Tony had managed to convince him.

'I can well imagine who might do it,' Tony said.

'Really? Who?'

'The man in a black coat.'

Dr Rummage pricked up his ears. 'The man in a black coat? Was the coat very long and full?'

Tony had a good idea what he was driving at, and took delight in leading him up the garden path.

'Yes, it stretched to the floor. It wasn't a proper coat, it was more like a cloak.'

'Really?' Dr Rummage whistled softly through his teeth. 'And what did the man look like?'

'He was very pale and had long straggly hair.'

'Did he smell all musty?' By now, Dr Rummage was really excited.

'I almost had to hold my nose,' Tony replied.

'Did you now?' said Dr Rummage. 'Where did you see this man?'

93

'In the barn. I happened to be looking when he disappeared among the straw bales.'

He had to really take a grip on himself in order not to laugh. Dr Rummage seemed to believe every word of it!

'What time of day did you see him?'

'It was dusk.' That of course was the only possible answer if he wanted Dr Rummage to believe it was a vampire he had seen. 'Could you show me the place where he disappeared?' asked Dr Rummage in barely contained excitement.

'Of course.'

As Tony moved away, he gave one look back at the old pigsty.

What would they do without me? he thought.

24

Vampire Verses

Of course Dr Rummage did not find any man in the barn. His dog merely stumbled on a couple of cats who sat in a box and miaowed pitifully.

Now Tony was in bed, and he was just thinking back over events with delight, when someone tapped softly on his window. He ran over and pushed the curtain aside. Outside sat Anna!

Startled, Tony opened the window. 'You can't stay here!' he cried. 'Mum's coming in a minute!'

'I only wanted to bring you my autograph book,' she replied with a smile, handing him the red book. 'Will you write in it?'

'Yes,' he said, feeling embarrassed – and then there was a knock on his door.

Immediately he heard his mother's horrified voice. 'Tony! Do you want to catch bronchitis?'

'I – er – I was so hot,' stuttered Tony, stuffing the autograph book down his pyjama trousers.

'You're feeling hot because you've got a temperature!' scolded his mother, shutting the window so quickly that she did not notice the small shadow which shrank into the corner. 'Have you taken your temperature?'

'Yes,' nodded Tony, and went slowly back to

his bed. I only hope the book doesn't fall out of my trousers! he thought.

Luckily his mother was busy with the thermometer. '100°!' she exclaimed.

By now Tony had reached the bed and let himself sink down into the soft mattress in relief. 'Is that high?' he asked innocently.

'You'll have to stay in bed tomorrow,' she told him. 'And now, put your light out and go to sleep.'

'Yes, Mum,' he said, and switched off the light.

'Not while I'm still in the room!' said his mother crossly, as she felt her way in the darkness to the door.

'Then may I put it on again?' he asked with a grin. But she snapped the door shut behind her without saying another word.

Tony waited till she had gone downstairs. Then he turned on the light and took out the autograph book. It had a red velvet cover which was already torn in a few places. A musty smell came from the material which reminded him of Anna. Was she still crouching on the window-sill?

He went to the window and peered outside, but there was no one to be seen. He went back to bed again and turned the first page in great anticipation.

THIS AUTOGRAPH BOOK BELONGS TO ANNA EMILY SACKVILLE-BAGG it said in a child's round handwriting, and underneath:

If a poem you complete,
Please be sure to keep it neat.

This request had obviously not been much help, for already the second page was covered in ink blots.

Life is at its best for me,
When blood doth flow in quantity.

Written to remind you of your brother, Gregory.

Tony flicked over a few more pages.

If in life you wish to find
True happiness of heart and mind,
Then drink the blood of mortal man
To give you joy, as well it can.

In memory of your Aunt Dorothy.

Tony felt himself shudder pleasantly. It was fun to read these bloodthirsty verses, and yet to know that the vampires who had written them were flying about outside and could do nothing to him. He read on avidly.

If e'er you hear the sound of song
Look there for blood, you won't be wrong!

This advice comes to you from your grandmother, Sabina the Sinister.

There then followed Rudolph's poem which Tony knew already, with the signature: A souvenir from your brother, Rudolph the Rotten. Tony had never before heard this nickname of Rudolph's, and he supposed that Rudolph had used it just to make himself sound important. Nearly all the vampires seemed to have a nickname: for example, William the Wild, whose verse stood on the following page:

Come rain or come sunshine,
Fire, wind, hail or flood,
Take care that on your lips
There's always fresh blood!

In memory of your grandfather.

The following page boasted a large spot of blood. Underneath was written:

White swan swimming on blue lake:
Dearest Anna, for my sake,
Keep your blood as fresh and pure
As swan's plumage, evermore.

So writes your Uncle Theodore.

Uncle Theodore! He was the vampire who had sat playing cards on his coffin and had been observed doing so by McRookery the Nightwatchman! Since that day, his coffin in the Sackville-Bagg family vault had lain empty . . . . That made the spot of blood even more grisly, thought Tony.

Quickly, he turned the page.

> *Conversing is silver:*
> *But bleeding is gold.*

So writes your father, Frederick the Frightful.

Back home in my autograph book, there are
only the most boring, or sensible, or stupid
rhymes, Tony thought enviously. There aren't
any that would give you the creeps! Not like
the one written in an ancient, twirly handwriting by Thelma the Thirsty:

> *Keep your teeth polished and keep your teeth nice.*
> *'Twill make you both healthy and wealthy and wise.*

To remind you of your mother.

The rest of the pages were empty – except
for one little word, 'Tony,' which Anna had
written at the top of the next page. If only he
knew what to write! But the only rhymes he
could think of were as boring as the ones in his
own autograph book.

'Roses are red, violets are blue, tulips are
yellow,' he murmured out loud, and tried
desperately to think of something to rhyme.

'Primroses too?' That wasn't very witty.

'What colour are you?' Not much better!

'How do you do?' No, that didn't work.

Tony sighed. It was going to be hard work,

thinking up a suitable verse! He took a notepad and pencil out of his bedside table drawer.

'A little house of roses, a little door of pinks . . .' he wrote, and then quickly crossed it out.

'Be like a little violet, Modest, good always, And not like other vampires, Always wanting praise . . . .' That sounded a bit better, but the vampires might be insulted by it. He would rather not risk that!

'Always be dutiful, always be wise, following always your parents' advice, Learn when to keep silent, when to speak out, There's a time and a place, of that there's no doubt.'

Tony's eyes began to close. For him, the time and the place had come to go to sleep – once he had hidden Anna's autograph book in his suitcase.

25

Dr Rummage's Discovery

When Tony woke up the next morning, there was a breakfast tray by his bed. Did his mother really think he was too ill to get up for breakfast? His throat still hurt, it was true, as he took his first sip of cocoa, but that would soon stop once he was up. He certainly did not want to stay in bed! What was more, he must find out whether any more excitements were in store for tonight.

He got dressed and went downstairs. His parents were at table, and they looked up in surprise as he came in. The two other ladies had presumably already had breakfast, for their places had been cleared away.

'You should be in bed!' said Tony's mother reproachfully.

'But I'm not ill.'

'Have you taken your temperature?' asked his father.

'Yes,' he lied.

'And what was it?'

'98°'

His parents exchanged looks. 'I don't believe it!' declared his mother. 'You look pale, and your eyes are too bright, just like yesterday.'

'I'm not ill!' said Tony furiously.

'Well, if you say so –' His mother sounded hurt. 'Would you like a roll?'

I – I'm not hungry, was what Tony nearly

said, but of course he must not admit that. 'Thank you.'

His father spread a roll with jam and gave it to him.

'Anyway – did Dr Rummage find the thief?' inquired Tony cautiously.

His mother looked at him significantly. 'No. But he did find something else – something that will be of interest to you, I should think!' she added pointedly.

Tony went even more pale. 'What?'

She pointed to an old, well-thumbed book which lay on the window-seat.

'That's yours, isn't it?'

It was *Voices from the Vault* which he had lent the Little Vampire a few week earlier!

'Where did you get that from?'

'It was in the henhouse. Dr Rummage discovered it behind a couple of boxes.'

'But . . .' said Tony, and then stopped. There was no point in explaining to them that he had lent the book to someone, because then they would immediately ask, who to!

'So we were right!' said his father.

'Yes. The book belongs to me.'

'Then we were right, too, that you had been in the henhouse?'

If only they knew! He wouldn't set foot in the henrun again for all the tea in China! But of course, he couldn't say that! So he lied. 'Yes.'

'Aha!' said his father, obviously satisfied. 'And while you were there, you . . . er . . . you played around a bit with the eggs.'

'What?' retorted Tony angrily. 'I'm still supposed to have mucked around with the eggs, am I? I never touched them!'

'Oh really?' countered his father coolly. 'Then who was it?'

Tony was so livid at the stubbornness and prejudice of his father that he forgot to be cautious. 'If you must know, it was the Little Vampire!' And with that, he ran out of the door.

At first, he wanted to go to his room, but then he realised his parents would certainly follow him there in order to talk to him. And he hadn't the slightest desire to be cross-examined any further! Then he remembered that in the barn there were two old bicycles, which guests were allowed to use. Yes, that's what he'd do: just ride off – and his parents, who always wanted to know where he was going, would have a real fright! Perhaps then they would realise how mean and unjust it was to suspect me! he thought, as he rode off on a green bicycle with no bell or brakes in the direction of Onionton. But he never got that far. Even after only a short way, he had to get off because he felt so dizzy. He stood by the bicycle uncertainly. Should he go on on foot?

But then he decided he did not feel like running away any more. He was suddenly so tired . . . . So he brought the bike back to the barn and went to his room.

26

A Visit

'He's got a temperature of 100.9°!' he heard his mother saying.

'Then we must call a doctor!' That was his father's voice.

Tony blinked. He saw his parents standing by the bed. They looked down at him in some concern.

'Am I ill?' he asked.

'Yes. We're going to call the doctor.'

'No, I don't want a doctor!' screamed Tony. His parents could not know who was the doctor here in the village.

'Why ever not?'

'Because . . . I'm feeling much better!'

'So suddenly?' said his mother in disbelief. 'No, I think the doctor had better take a look at you.'

'You've never been frightened of doctors before,' remarked his father in some amazement.

'It's never before been . . .' said Tony. 'Well, never been some idiot village doctor before!'

'Tony!' cried his mother. 'Whatever has got into you?'

'It's true though!' he said. 'Here in the village, I bet they can't tell the difference between a syringe and a pitchfork!'

'I think you're hallucinating!' said his father irritably.

'I only hope so!' growled Tony.

But unfortunately Dr Rummage was no figment of his imagination when he came and stood by his bed shortly afterwards. No, he was all too real with his broad face and piercing blue eyes.

'So you're ill, are you?' he asked in a clumsily friendly voice.

'I dunno,' was all Tony would say.

'You don't know?' Dr Rummage sounded amused.

Tony had already decided to be as unhelpful as possible. 'I dunno what Mum's been telling you!'

'Tony, please!' protested his mother.

'Well, open your mouth,' said Dr Rummage, looking in his little black bag.

Reluctantly Tony did as he was told.

'His throat is inflamed,' announced Dr Rummage when he had peered into Tony's mouth. 'You must really have caught a cold yesterday evening.' Tony blushed.

'Did you find that piece of paper by the way?' Dr Rummage went on. It did not seem to bother him that Tony could not answer, as he was still keeping his mouth open. 'Little boys should not wander about alone in the dark,' he remarked, as he sprayed a stinging liquid down Tony's throat. 'Who knows who might be out and about? Although in fact I never caught a glimpse of the man you were telling me about.'

'What man?' asked Tony's father, suddenly alert. Tony would have liked to have sunk

through the floor! He'd been waiting for this question!

'Don't you know?' said Dr Rummage in surprise 'There was meant to be some man hiding in the barn. He was very pale, had long straggly hair and was wearing a black cloak.'

'Did Tony tell you that?' asked his mother.

'Yes.'

'He just made it up!' she exclaimed. 'He must have read about it in one of his crazy books!'

All eyes turned on Tony.

'Is that true?' asked his father. 'Did you make it up?'

'Yes,' admitted Tony after a slight hesitation.

'But why?' aked Dr Rummage.

'To make himself seem important!' replied his father.

Tony bit his lips. It was a mean suggestion – and yet he could not defend himself without giving away the Little Vampire!

'I wanted to play a trick on you,' he said through clenched teeth.

'Nice kind of trick!' remarked Dr Rummage grimly. 'And presumably the real egg-thief got away because of it!'

Tony had to smile. If only Dr Rummage knew how right he was!

'I thought you'd known for a long time who's been stealing the eggs,' he said innocently.

'What do you mean?'

'Well . . . my father knows who the culprit is, don't you, Dad?'

107

'What are you talking about?' exclaimed his father angrily.

'Isn't it true that you suspect someone?'

'And who might that be?' His father had even turned a little pink, Tony noticed with secret satisfaction.

'Yes, who?' asked Dr Rummage excitedly.

Tony smiled. 'Me,' he said smoothly.

'What nonsense!' exclaimed his father turning to Dr Rummage. 'I only wanted to know how his book had got into the henhouse!'

'Don't fight, please!' pleaded Mum. 'After all, Tony is unwell.'

'Exactly!' said Tony. 'And now I need some rest!' With that, he lay back on his pillows and shut his eyes – although not so tightly that he could not see Dr Rummage snap his bag shut.

'I'll drop by again in the morning,' he said.

When he had gone, Tony's mother said: 'Now you won't be able to have fun with us, this evening.'

'I didn't much want to anyway,' grunted Tony.

'Even so, it's a pity. How typical to go and get ill while we're on holiday!'

'It's not my fault!' muttered Tony, and turned to face the wall.

27

Get Better Soon!

At half past eight, as the smell of sausages being grilled in the garden reached Tony's room, someone knocked softly on the door.

'Yes?' he said.

Joanna came in, with a paper plate and a mug in her hand. 'I thought you might be hungry,' she said and put the things down on his bedside table. As she did so, her glance fell on Anna's autograph book which was also lying there.

'Is that a book about vampires?' she asked curiously.

'No,' said Tony hastily, stuffing the book under his pillow. 'It's an autograph book.'

'An autograph book?' Joanna giggled. 'Round here, only girls write in autograph books!'

'Boys are more open-minded where I live!'

'May I look at it?'

'No.'

'Oh please!'

'All I can do is read a couple of rhymes out to you,' said Tony with a malicious grin.

'Oh yes!'

Tony took out the book and held it so that she would not be able to see the pages. 'Life is at its best for me, when blood doth flow in quantity!'

Joanna's eyes were wide open. 'Does it really say that?'

'Do you want to hear another?' he asked with a slight laugh, and without waiting for her answer, he read: 'Come rain or come sunshine, Fire, wind, hail or flood, Take care that on your lips, There's always fresh blood!'

'Eeeugh! What horrible rhymes!' cried Joanna. 'I'd rather not have them in my autograph book!'

Tony grinned. 'Some people like them!'

'Who does the book belong to then?'

'It . . . it belongs to my girlfriend.'

'Your girlfriend?' asked Joanna in astonishment. 'I didn't know you had a –'

'You can't know everything,' he said.

'Do I know her?'

'Of course not.'

'What's her name?'

'Anna.'

'Oh well,' she said in embarrassment, going to the door. 'Get better soon!'

'Thanks for the food!' Tony called after her.

28

Tulips, Snowdrops Bloom in Spring!

Joanna had hardly closed the door behind her when someone knocked on the window. Tony waited till her footsteps had died away. Then he got up and went quietly over to the window. He pulled the curtain to one side and peered out.

At first, all he could see was the dark night sky and the moon. But then he saw something else – Anna's face! She was sitting on the window-sill and had drawn her cloak tightly round her, as though she were freezing cold.

Tony opened the window.

'May I come in?' she asked.

'If you like,' he said, irritated that his voice should sound so quivery.

'Of course I like!' she smiled and sprang lightly into the room. She looked around and said: 'You had a visitor!'

'How do you know?'

'I heard you.'

Tony felt himself go red. 'Did you hear what we were talking about?'

'Yes. You told her I was your girlfriend!'

'I only said that because she wanted to know who the autograph book belonged to!' he tried to make an excuse. He found it extremely painful that she should have heard it all!

But Anna did not seem to find anything

wrong. 'It doesn't matter if she knows about us,' she said casually, as if it were the most natural thing in the world. Then she went over to the bed where the autograph book lay. 'Have you written in it?'

'No. I can't think of anything.'

'But there are so many rhymes! Shall I tell you one?

Tulips, snowdrops bloom in Spring!
Mother may know everything.
Just one secret keep from view –
When a boy first kisses you!

She broke into fits of giggles, but Tony merely raised an eyebrow.

'I'm not writing anything like that!' he declared.

'Why aren't you down in the garden, anyway?' she asked suddenly. 'There's a party going on.'

'Don't feel like it,' grunted Tony, who did not want her to find out about his sore throat and start being sorry for him.

'But it looks a great party!' she enthused. 'There's a huge bonfire, and lanterns hanging in the trees . . .'

'. . . It's just for little kids!' he said disparagingly.

'No. There are grown-ups there too! I'd like to go and join in, anyway.'

'Why don't you then?'

'I'm not that stupid!' she retorted. 'Anyway, there isn't time. I've got to help Rudolph take his coffin back to the vault.'

'You're taking his coffin back to the vault?' exclaimed Tony in dismay. 'But why?'

'Because of Dr Rummage. Rudolph hasn't been able to sleep a wink all day, and now all he wants to do is go home.'

'Why didn't he tell me all this himself?'

'Because he's scared. Actually he thinks Dr Rummage is sitting out there in the garden!'

'But he'll never find his way back without me!'

'You think so?' said Anna haughtily. 'He's got me! I'm very good at finding my way in the dark. And I did manage to get here, after all!'

'But you don't know the dangers of the countryside! There are lots of people round here who do believe in vampires!'

Anna looked at him tenderly. 'Are you worried about me?'

'I . . . just don't want anything to happen to you, that's all,' he stuttered.

Anna's large eyes glittered. 'Ah, Tony,' she sighed, and quickly turned her head away. 'No one's ever been worried about me before,' she said quietly.

Tony coughed in embarrassment. 'I could take you to the station,' he said, to turn the conversation to a less tricky subject. 'From there, you can fly following the railway line.'

'It's really not necessary!' she protested.

'Even so,' said Tony, 'three people achieve more than two!'

'All right then!' she said, and, looking steadily at him, she added: 'And at least we two will be together for a bit longer!'

'We . . . we ought to get going!' he murmured.

'In your pyjamas?' she said with a laugh.

Tony looked down with a start. For the first time, he noticed he was wearing his pyjamas in front of Anna – his awful old crumpled, baggy pyjamas!

Anna seemed to sense his embarrassment. She climbed up to the window and said: 'We'll wait for you at the pigsty.' And then she was gone.

29

News from the Vault

Tony put on his thickest pullover and tied a
scarf round his neck. His sore throat felt
rather worse, in spite of the pills Dr Rummage
had given him. They were probably the wrong
kind! he thought spitefully, pills for an upset
stomach or athlete's foot! Even so, he popped
another in his mouth before he went downstairs.

He stopped at the front door and listened.
Luckily the garden was on the other side of the
house. He could hear the sound of music
wafting over, and also a woman laughing. He
hoped the party would go on for quite a while
– at least until he was back from the station!
And if it didn't? Well, he'd think up some
excuse.

Anna and Rudolph were waiting for him at
the door of the pigsty, in the shadow of which
they had laid the coffin.

'Here you are at last!' growled the vampire.

'Don't be so mean to Tony!' Anna scolded
him. 'After all, he is trying to help you.'

'I know, I know. First he talks me into
coming here, and now I'm supposed to be
grateful to him!'

'I talked you into coming, did I?' cried Tony
angrily. 'And who had to get away from
George the Boisterous?'

The vampire gave a broad grin. 'No one. In

115

fact, George the Boisterous has left the vault!'

Tony gasped in indignation at the way the Little Vampire had twisted the facts yet again. 'That's not true!'

'Isn't it?' smiled the vampire. 'Ask Anna whether he's left or not!'

'I don't mean that!' cried Tony furiously. Of course Rudolph knew exactly what Tony was talking about, but he was so obstinate that he would never admit it. And it was pointless to quarrel with him now.

'He really has left,' said Anna, who could not know what all the fuss was about. 'George the Boisterous wanted the tie-pin back that he had given to Greg, but Greg didn't want to give it to him so he threw him out of the vault!' She giggled.

'You see!' exulted the vampire. 'So now you can help Anna carry the coffin.'

'And what will you do?' asked Anna.

'I'll show you the way.'

'That would just suit you, wouldn't it? Either you carry the front end, or I won't carry it at all!'

'What about Tony?' protested the vampire.

'Tony will show us the way!' she declared, and went to the back of the coffin.

'Well? Is the coffin going to stay here?'

'I'm coming,' grumbled the vampire grudgingly, and picked up the front end.

'We're ready!' she smiled at Tony, who had just checked once more that no one was about.

'Good!' he said. 'The coast is clear!'

30

Low Blood Pressure

They went round the barn and across the yard, in which Tony's parents' car and the pale blue minibus belonging to the Herrings were parked. Once through the tall trees beyond, and they had reached the road to the village. After they had been walking for a while, the Little Vampire put down his end of the coffin.

'My back aches!' he groaned.

'You only want Tony to carry the coffin for you!' scolded Anna.

'But I haven't slept all day,' he complained, 'and I haven't eaten either! I'm getting black spots in front of my eyes!'

'Pull the other one,' was all she said.

'I've got low blood pressure!' cried the Little Vampire. 'So I might easily faint!'

'Really?' asked Anna disbelievingly. 'And how are you supposed to know you have low blood pressure?'

'I can feel it.'

'And I can feel you're just a lazy beast!' she retorted crossly.

The vampire made a hurt face. 'That's not for you to judge. After all, you're still half a baby.'

'That's what you think, Grandpa!' answered Anna, letting her end of the coffin bump down on Rudolph's foot.

'Have you gone bonkers?' hissed Tony.

'You're making enough noise to wake the whole neighbourhood!'

That brought Rudolph and Anna up short. Suddenly they were still as mice.

'Has anyone heard us?' asked the Little Vampire worriedly.

Tony nodded in the direction of a house which lay hidden behind a hedge; all that could be seen of it was a lighted attic window. 'Quite possibly . . . .'

'We must go on,' urged Anna.

'No, wait,' said the vampire. 'Perhaps I could get some strength up from in there first . . . .'

'I wouldn't,' advised Anna.

'I would!' retorted the vampire. 'And then I'll find carrying the coffin so much easier . . . .'

With half-open lips and a staring, vacant look in his eyes, he crept slowly up to the house. Anna hastily pulled the coffin behind a bush.

'Come on, we'd better follow him,' she whispered to Tony. 'Otherwise there'll be another disaster!'

31

Spies

The Little Vampire went up the carefully raked path to the house like a sleep-walker, followed by Tony and Anna. It was a modern, red-brick house with a front door made of metal and glass, over which a small light glowed. The windows on the ground floor were dark. Only up at one of the attic windows was a light burning.

The Little Vampire did not stop to investigate the front of the house. He went purposefully round to the back.

'He thinks everybody forgets to lock the back door,' said Tony softly to Anna.

She looked at him in astonishment. 'Is that true?'

'No. But he'll find out himself soon enough.'

'Shouldn't we follow him?'

'I'd rather stay here behind these bushes,' answered Tony. 'Anyway, he's bound to come straight back.'

After a moment, Anna remarked: 'I'd love just to have a look at what it's like inside. I'm very interested in interior decoration.'

'Do you mean you want to go inside?'

'No, just peek through the windows,' she said. 'Will you wait for me?'

Tony nodded. She quickly ran over to the house and peered in through the windows. She came back looking disappointed.

'Pooh, it's very boring,' she said. 'In the left-hand room, there's just a dining table and four chairs. In the room on the right, there's a desk near the door and apart from that, only bookshelves.'

Tony yawned, just to show he was not at all interested.

'And next door is the living-room,' she went on. 'With a sofa, a table and two armchairs. Oh yes, and there's a glass cupboard against the wall.' Tony was only half listening but he gave a start when she said: 'And in the glass cupboard there are lots and lots of butterflies!'

'What did you say were in the glass cupboard?' he asked. 'Butterflies?'

'Yes. I could see them clearly, because the moon was shining into the room. And just imagine – someone has pinned them through with matchsticks!'

'Oh no!' Tony groaned. 'It's Dr Rummage's house!' Anna's eyes widened in fright.

'Dr Rummage's house? And Rudolph . . . .'

'Let's just hope the back door was locked,' said Tony gloomily.

Just then, they heard a furious barking coming from the back of the house.

Tony jumped.

'Dr Rummage's dog! The black monster!'

'I'll go and see if anything's happened to Rudolph!' declared Anna, turning to go.

'Wait!' called Tony, holding firmly onto her cloak.

Impatiently she asked: 'Well, have you got a better idea?'

'We mustn't do anything rash!' he said imploringly. 'Or do you want Dr Rummage to get his hands on you too?'

'Do you think . . .?' She left the sentence unfinished, for at that moment, a light went on in the right-hand room, the consulting room. And what they saw inside took their breath away. Dr Rummage came into the room – pushing in front of him the Little Vampire!

Rudolph's head was bowed, like an animal being led to the slaughter.

'Oh how terrible!' whispered Anna. 'What's he going to do to him?'

As if he had heard her words, Dr Rummage pulled the curtains shut with a jerk.

'First he'll sound him out,' suggested Tony.

'Yes, but then what . . . .'

Tony said no more, the thought was too dreadful. He had seen only too clearly the sharpened stakes of wood protruding from Dr Rummage's jacket pocket . . . .

'I'd like to smash the window!' said Anna, shaking her tiny fists.

'That wouldn't be any use,' answered Tony. 'We'll have to do something else, something crafty. And I think I know what . . . .'

'What?' breathed Anna, her eyes wide open.

'I'll go and ring the bell. Then Dr Rummage will come to the door . . .'

'. . . and Rudolph can escape!' she finished excitedly. 'Oh Tony, I'm scared!'

So am I, thought Tony, but decided it was better not to say so. He stuck out his chin in determination and marched confidently up to the front door. He felt rather like a bull fighter on his way to the arena.

'Good luck!' Anna called after him.

'Thanks!' he said softly, and pressed the doorbell.

32

Not my Consulting Time

Tony heard the bell ring inside the house. To his ears it sounded shrill and discordant, and his heart began to pound. But nothing moved. He gulped. Then he rang a second time. Footsteps came towards him. Tony would have liked to have turned and run, but he thought of the Little Vampire and gritted his teeth.

Dr Rummage opened the door, but only an inch. He looked at Tony distrustfully through narrowed eyes. 'What do you want?' he asked gruffly.

'I . . .' Tony had thought out beforehand exactly what to say, but under Dr Rummage's piercing gaze, he still ended up stuttering. 'I . . . it's about my . . . my sore throat!'

Dr Rummage's forbidding expression lightened. 'Oh I see! Yes, now I recognise you. You're the boy on holiday who's got a bad throat.' He opened the door a little wider. 'But tell me, what are you doing out here? Why aren't you in bed?'

'My . . . my mother sent me,' lied Tony. 'I'm – I'm supposed to fetch some different pills. The ones you gave me don't help.'

'Of course they don't help if you're up and about all the time!' said Dr Rummage crossly. 'But I will give you some more, nonetheless. Wait here!'

'J-just a minute!' called Tony. He noticed he was coming out in a sweat. At all costs, he must keep Dr Rummage at the door for a bit longer if the Little Vampire was going to manage to escape. 'My-my mother also said you should take another look at my sore throat!'

'And that's why she sent you over here in the cold night air?' Dr Rummage shook his head. 'What stupidity! If I didn't have a visitor, I would call your mother and ask her to come and fetch you! But as I say, I've got a visitor...' he continued in quite a different voice, looking nervously behind him, as if he expected the Little Vampire to appear. Hopefully he had long since made his escape!

He went on crossly: 'It isn't my consulting time now! And also I must go and attend to my visitor! Come back tomorrow morning.'

Tony took his courage in both hands. 'What about my pills?'

Dr Rummage was obviously getting twitchy. 'I'll fetch you a couple from my consulting room,' he said. 'Wait here.'

Anxiously, Tony watched him disappear into the room. For a moment, he heard nothing. Then there was uproar!

'The window! I never thought of that...'

Tony gave a little jump for joy. Now he could be sure that the Little Vampire had made his escape. But he himself preferred not to meet Dr Rummage at this very moment....

He quickly turned and raced away. He ran down the garden path and pulled the gate shut behind him. Only when he reached the bush where Anna had hidden the coffin did he stop.

But there was nothing there! No trace of Anna, or the Little Vampire! Only the flattened grass showed where the coffin had lain.

Should he go on alone to the station in the hope of meeting Anna and Rudolph on the way? No! The two vampires could manage quite well without him. He drew the scarf more tightly round his neck, and ran back to the farm.

33

If Your Mother's Still Around

Tony approached the farmhouse with an uneasy feeling. He strained his ears to listen, but no music came from the garden any longer: no murmur of voices, no laughter. Had the party finished already?

He noticed that a light was on in his room, but it might have been that he had forgotten to switch it off. The front door was not locked. As he crept quietly up the stairs, he could hear that the television was on. Please let them all be sitting downstairs watching a film! he prayed.

But as he cautiously opened the door of his room, the first thing he saw was his mother sitting on a chair by his bed.

'Hallo, Mum!' he said, as charmingly as he could.

She said nothing, but the corner of her mouth twitched.

'Have you been here long?' He quickly slipped into his pyjamas and got into bed.

'Where were you?' she asked sharply. Her voice sounded so angry that he winced.

'At the doctor's,' he replied truthfully.

'I'm supposed to believe that, am I?'

'You can ring him up.'

'And what in the world were you doing there?'

'I wanted to get some different pills.'

'You wanted . . .' She stopped. She obviously had not been prepared for that. 'And I thought you were flitting about outside looking for vampires!'

'But Mum!' he said, 'I'm not as mad as that!'

His mother studied him suspiciously. 'Were you really with Dr Rummage?'

'Yes!'

'Why didn't you tell us? We'd have gone to fetch the pills for you.'

'I didn't want to bother you,' he said craftily. His mother was particularly keen on politeness! 'And fresh air is healthy – that's what you keep telling me, anyway.'

'Did you get the pills?'

'The pills? N-no. Dr Rummage had – er – had another patient with him. But anyway, I don't need them any more, I'm almost better.'

'It's a pretty muddled story,' said his mother, 'but just because of that, I believe it.'

Tony made a reproachful face. 'Why shouldn't it be true? Do you think I'd lie to you?' And it really was not a made-up story . . . Tony had just left out the bits his mother must not know about!

'When are we leaving exactly?' he asked, to divert her attention. He hoped it would be before Dr Rummage came to see him!

'Straight after breakfast,' replied his mother. 'Dad's got to be back in the office in the afternoon.'

Tony could have hugged her! But he must not let her see that, of course! 'What a pity,' he said in pretended disappointment.

129

'Have you enjoyed yourself here then?' she asked in surprise.

'Yes,' he lied.

'Didn't you miss all your vampires?'

'Wh-what do you mean?'

'Your funny friends who go around in vampire cloaks?'

'Not at all,' Tony assured her. How could I have missed them? he thought with a grin.

'If that's the case, we could come back here soon for another holiday on the farm!'

'That suits me!' he said evenly. He could not have cared less what the future held in store at that moment.

'It's only your vampire books that you couldn't give up!' his mother remarked cuttingly.

'What do you mean?'

'You were in a great hurry to buy yourself one in that little shop.'

'So?'

'And you brought *Voices from the Vault* with you from home.'

'If that's what you think.'

'And I've found another vampire book you've hidden!'

Tony blanched. 'Really? Which one's that?'

With a triumphant smile, his mother produced from behind her back Anna's autograph book. '*Vampire Verses!*' she said, looking at the book with disgust.

'Have you looked in it?' exclaimed Tony indignantly.

'Of course.' She opened it. 'Anna Emily

Sackville-Bagg – is she a girl at your school? Her name seems familiar somehow.'

'She – she's in the second form.'

Tony's mother leafed through the book. 'She's thought up some peculiar names in here! William the Wild, Frederick the Frightful . . . are they meant to be funny?' With a shake of her head, she read: "Take care that on your lips There's always fresh blood!" In my day we only wrote *nice* verses!'

'Times have changed,' said Tony, who was delighted that she did not seem to be taking the verses seriously.

She shut the book with a snap and handed it to him. 'And what will you write in it?'

Tony gave a broad grin.

> *'If your mother's still around*
> *Be grateful through and through*
> *Lots of people in this world*
> *Are not so lucky as you!'*

His mother was well aware of the sarcasm hidden in his voice as he said this verse. She stood up. 'You really must be almost well again!' she said irritably, and left the room.

Tony gave the autograph book a last glance, but he was too tired to think of another rhyme. He could do it tomorrow – on the journey home.

34

Sharing the Work

Tony brought down to breakfast the case and school satchel in which he had hidden the vampire books and the cloak. He carried Anna's autograph book quite openly under his arm – there was no need to hide that any more.

In the dining room, he found his mother. She was sitting at table, had a cup of coffee in front of her and was talking to the two ladies.

'Last night we slept really well for the very first time!' said one.

The other agreed with her. 'It was blissfully quiet! What a shame you have to leave right now!'

'Yes, a real pity!' remarked Tony.

'Tony has radically changed his opinion of farms,' explained his mother proudly. 'Isn't that so, Tony? You have had fun after all.'

'Certainly have,' he said, without much risk, because out of the window he could see his father loading up the car.

'Unfortunately it's the end of the school holidays once again,' said his mother.

'Unfortunately's the right word!' Tony agreed with her wholeheartedly. Then something occurred to him. 'Do I absolutely have to go back to school?'

'Why ever shouldn't you?'

'Well, I am ill, after all.'

'So you're ill are you? Then we'd better wait

and see Dr Rummage.'

'Er – I'm not that ill!' he assured her hastily. 'In fact, I'm quite well really.' That was not completely true, but he certainly did not want to meet Dr Rummage again! 'I can even take my case out to the car by myself. And my satchel too.'

With those words, he gathered up his luggage and quickly left the room, before his mother could remind him that he still had not eaten anything.

He put down his case next to the car.

'Are we leaving soon?' he asked.

'Can you still not wait?' grinned his father.

'On the contrary,' said Tony. As he was certain it would not be possible, he added cheekily: 'If it were up to me, we'd stay here for another week!'

His father seemed to take him seriously. 'Sadly I've got to be back at the office this afternoon,' he explained. 'So we really do have to leave – as soon as I'm ready.'

The sooner the better! thought Tony.

'Can I help you?' he asked cheerfully.

'You can let Mum know.'

He bumped into his mother at the front door.

'Just look what Joanna's found!' she said, showing Tony the hat she was holding. 'Isn't it just like yours? The same felt, the same green feather . . .'

Tony did his best not to give anything away. 'Yes – it's very similar –' Of course, it *was* his hat, the one the Little Vampire had lost!

'Where did she find it?' he asked.

'In with the horses, I think. Funny, it really could almost be your hat.' With that, she hung it by the coat hooks.

'Perhaps we should take it back with us,' suggested Tony. 'Just in case my hat ever goes missing . . . .'

His mother looked at him in surprise. 'I thought you didn't like Tyrolean hats?'

'Oh I do. Especially in winter –' It wasn't a very convincing explanation, he could see that for himself.

'One hat's enough,' his mother decided in any case. 'What's more, it doesn't belong to us. Whoever owns it will come and fetch it sooner or later.'

'As you like,' said Tony crossly. In that case it would be her fault when he could not produce it the next time he visited his granny who had given it to him! Just to irritate her, he asked: 'Anyway – why are you leaving Dad to do all the work? You're the one who's always so keen on a sharing of labour!'

She threw him a poisonous look. 'You would have to say something like that!'

He grinned. 'I'm not the one who's always for sharing the work – you are!' he declared, and walked over to the car, head held high.

Mrs Herring and Joanna were waiting for him.

'I'm so glad you have enjoyed your stay,' said Mrs Herring, without even asking him if he had. She looked at Joanna. 'And we'd be very pleased if you would come and stay again – wouldn't we?'

Joanna nodded – and then went red.

'Jeremy would be pleased too,' went on Mrs Herring. 'He's gone off to do the shopping with my husband today.'

'If your children would ever like to visit us, we would be delighted to have them,' said Tony's mother – also without having asked him!

'Oh yes!' enthused Joanna.

'Oh no!' groaned Tony.

'You mustn't take what Tony says too seriously,' said his mother. 'He's rather shy. What's more, he hasn't had anything to eat today and that's why he's so grumpy.' And she held out a package wrapped in greaseproof paper. 'Here. I've just made this for you. For the journey.'

'Thanks,' he growled, unwrapped a sandwich from the package and took a bite. That way, at least he would not be tempted to contradict anything and thus prolong the conversation any further.

'Can't we go yet?' he asked ungraciously.

'You see?' laughed his mother. 'He's always grumpy like this when his tummy's empty!'

35

Vampires and Other Friends

'You made me out to be impossible!' complained Tony once they were in the car.

'You think so?' said his mother, starting the engine.

Slowly they drove across the yard, past Mrs Herring and Joanna, who waved eagerly.

'Don't you agree, you were grumpy?' asked his father.

'I had reason to be!' Tony defended himself. 'Why you had to invite them without even asking me . . . .now I suppose they'll even have to sleep in my bedroom!'

'At least they're better than your vampire friends!' retorted his mother. 'And I think it's time you found yourself some more friends.'

'Well I don't!' said Tony defiantly.

Secretly, he had to admit she could be right. The Little Vampire really had not behaved as a friend should! Tony only had to think of how they had carried the coffin to the railway station together, and the vampire had never even said thank you at the end of it all! Or how Tony had practically saved his friend's life with the people who were waiting for their two holiday children from Manchester, and the vampire had just squabbled with him, instead of being grateful and pleased! Or how, whenever it came to George the Boisterous, the vampire simply twisted the facts to lay the blame on Tony!

You had to make allowances for the fact that as a vampire, he had a hard life and therefore had to think more of his own interests than a human would – but even so! Friendship meant that you did not just think of yourself, but of the other person occasionally . . . like Anna did!

Whereas he had felt only crossness and disappointment as he thought of Rudolph, at the thought of Anna a warm glow spread over him. He opened the autograph book and read the verses through again, one after the other. When he came to the page where 'Tony' was written in Anna's childish handwriting, he suddenly knew what to write.

'Have you got something to write with?' he asked.

His father handed him a biro, and he wrote:

In cold Siberia lives the brown bear.
Africa is the home of the gnu.
Sicily shelters the wild pig so rare –
But in my heart, there's room just for you!

In memory of your *friend*, Tony

He underlined the word 'friend' twice.

Contented and relieved, he leant back in his seat. The Little Vampire would be bound to see the poem – and he would get downright annoyed! And he might even get a bit more thoughtful, perhaps!

138

Tony's mother had been watching him in the driver's mirror. 'That autograph book with its stupid rhymes just proves that they aren't good friends for you to have,' she announced.

And his father asked: 'When did you last go to volleyball practice, by the way?'

Tony hesitated. 'About six months ago.'

'Wouldn't you like to start going again? You used to enjoy it!'

'Hmmm –'

'And what about your friend Olly?' asked his mother. 'Weren't you going to do a pottery course with him?'

'Yes, but –'

'Well then! And you can give that autograph book back to your friend with the vampire cloak as soon as possible!'

Tony grinned to himself. If only it were as simple as that . . . . But the idea of the pottery course did appeal to him suddenly. You could always model other things than flower vases – why not – vampires!

THE THREE DETECTIVES AND THE
MISSING SUPERSTAR

Simon Brett

0 590 70530 X   £1.25

It was quite by chance that Emma Cobbett saw
Dazzleman, lead singer of the chart-topping
group Reddimix, leave the studio where her
father was directing the group's new pro-
motional video. She didn't really want the
autograph the singer gave her before being
driven away, but when it seems clear that
Dazzleman has disappeared, everyone else
thinks it is an exasperatingly mistimed pub-
licity stunt. Emma has her doubts, especially
when she discovers that she didn't get an
autograph from Dazzleman at all, but a coded
message!

With her friends Stewi and Marcus, Emma
investigates the kidnapping of Dazzleman – a
crime that only the Three Detectives believe
has happened. As their enquiries continue –
helped by the irrepressible Kimberley, Dazzleman's most devoted fan – the Three Detectives
realise that the key to what they're dealing
with lies in Dazzleman's mysterious past – and
it's much more serious than it had seemed at
first.

THE LITTLE VAMPIRE TAKES A TRIP

Angela Sommer-Bodenburg

0 590 70408 7   £1.25

The idea of a family holiday in boring Nether Bogsbottom becomes more interesting to Tony when the Little Vampire agrees to come along. But how will they get the coffin there in secret . . .?

AM I GOING WITH YOU?

Thurley Fowler

0 590 70539 3   £1.25

' "Sydney, that's great."

"Not you dear. You can't go. This is my big chance to get into television. I'm sorry, Carlton, you just have to go to your Uncle Harry." '

Poor Carlton. Not only had he the burden of being named after a football team, but his mother was sending him away to his uncle while she went to Sydney. Carlton hated the farm and his cousin Simon. What if something happened to him at school? Who did you tell when your mother wasn't there?

Everything was different on the farm. From the moment he arrived he was in trouble. His uncle seemed to dislike him, his cousin tormented him. But life wasn't all black. On the cricket pitch he really came into his own. And eventually other things began to fall into place.

CRY VAMPIRE!

Terrance Dicks

0 590 70405 2   £1.25

Anna Markos had disappeared. The police had started a big hunt – but Simon and Sally knew they wouldn't find the young girl. They knew exactly where she was. But what could they do? Who on earth would believe them if they said she'd fallen into the clutches of vampires . . .?

THE BANGER BOYS

Anne Fussell

0 590 70536 9   £1.25

"A Word of advice . . ." said Mr Sampson the probation officer, ". . . keep away from your so-called mates. They're not the ones who ended up here today, and they're not the ones who will go to a detention centre next time."

Lol was lucky. He had been sentenced for stealing cars and had to spend time at the Sumner House Project. But when he got there he found that they expected him to work with a team to put together an old banger and maybe even drive her in a stock car race! The six months he spent going to Sumner House really changed things in Lol's life.

LAST SEEN ON HOPPER'S LANE

Janet Allais Stegeman

0 590 70435 4   £1.50

Kerry discovered the old, stone house on Hopper's Lane by chance and getting inside was not as hard as she thought it might be. Inside the air was cold and dead, like a tomb — the only sound was Kerry's own quick breathing.

Along the hallway was a drawing-room of such proportions that Kerry felt dwarfed, and in her mind's eye she imagined herself dressed in a dazzling gown, dancing to an orchestra. But as she waltzed and turned, Kerry's song choked to a terrified stop in her throat. There stood the ugliest little man she had ever seen, and he was pointing a gun at her.

"Don't move," he said. "And don't make a sound. Leave your hands up."

Kerry's whole body went rigid, her stomach heaved with fear.

"All right — walk in front of me!" And he jammed the point of the pistol in her back. "We're going to get in the van."

The back of the van was dim. Kerry was confused and frightened. But there was one thing of which Kerry was sure — she needed to get out of the van before it was too late . . . Kerry didn't want to be LAST SEEN ON HOPPER'S LANE!

And for Older Readers:

I WILL CALL IT GEORGIE'S BLUES

Suzanne Newton

0 590 70352 8   £1.95

Preacher's kids aren't any different to anyone else," I said stiffly.

"Maybe not, but they should be."

To the residents of Gideon, North Carolina, Neal, Aileen and Georgie Sloan constitute the "perfect" minister's family. But life for the children of Richard Sloan is tougher than it looks, and the happy public face hides the strains and secrets that are forcing the family apart.

Neal finds himself in an impossible position; trying to please his relentlessly strict father, struggling to remain friends with his rebellious older sister – who is in danger of failing to graduate from High School to the shame of the family – and trying to win the trust of and reassure his little brother Georgie, who suffers from his own dark and engulfing fears. Neal is forced to keep his own passion for playing jazz piano a close secret between himself and their neighbour, Mrs Talbot, for without this release he fears for his own stability. But Georgie is the catalyst. Seams begin to unravel in the perfect family fabric until catastrophe forces Georgie over the edge of sanity.